I0583665

BONDED TO THE BERSERKERS

A MENAGE SHIFTER ROMANCE

LEE SAVINO

FREE BOOK

Get a secret Berserker book, Bred by the Berserkers (only to
the awesomesauce fans on Lee's email list)
Go here to get started... https://geni.us/BredBerserker

BONDED TO THE BERSERKERS

I am an orphan, locked away in the abbey. Men call me beautiful, but I am destined for a life working in the kitchens --until the Berserkers capture me.

These Viking warriors are cursed, but my heart beats faster in their presence. My insides grow weak, desire filling me like fine wine. They draw wicked feelings from me and make me yearn for more.

I long to escape, but deep down, I know I'll never be free.

I belong to the Berserkers, and they to me.

Author's Note: Bonded to the Berserkers is a standalone, full-length MFM ménage romance starring two huge, dominant warriors who make it all about the woman. Read the whole best-selling Berserker saga to see what readers are raving about...

***

The Berserker Saga

Sold to the Berserkers - – Brenna, Samuel & Daegan
Mated to the Berserkers - – Brenna, Samuel & Daegan
Bred by the Berserkers (FREE novella only available at
www.leesavino.com) - – Brenna, Samuel & Daegan
Taken by the Berserkers – Sabine, Ragnvald & Maddox
Given to the Berserkers – Muriel and her mates
Claimed by the Berserkers – Fleur and her mates

Berserker Brides

Rescued by the Berserker – Hazel & Knut
Captured by the Berserkers – Willow, Leif & Brokk
Kidnapped by the Berserkers – Sage, Thorbjorn & Rolf
Bonded to the Berserkers – Laurel, Haakon & Ulf
Berserker Babies – the sisters Brenna, Sabine, Muriel, Fleur
and their mates
Night of the Berserkers – the witch Yseult's story
Owned by the Berserkers – Fern, Dagg & Svein
Tamed by the Berserkers — Sorrel, Thorsteinn & Vik
Mastered by the Berserkers - coming in 2020, Juliet and her
mates

Berserker Warriors

Aegir (formerly titled *The Sea Wolf*)
Siebold - coming in 2020

LAUREL

The first scream came from the dormitory. It came loud and clear, ringing through the kitchen where I stood with my arms elbow-deep in soapy water.

"Curses," I muttered, grabbing a cloth to dry my hands. Who was awake and shouting at this late hour? Which one of the orphans had cried out? We all knew to stay quiet, even when being punished.

Sage rushed in from the back hall. She was my age, but small and frail, and much too thin.

"What is it? What is happening?" I asked.

"Somebody cried out," she said. "One of the girls must be having a nightmare."

That couldn't be it. No orphan would dare. Sage's creased forehead told me she shared my thoughts.

Footsteps stomped up the hall—the friar coming to investigate. He would be angry at being disturbed. I'd drugged his draught that night, but obviously not enough.

Out of habit, I grabbed the mead jug, ready to refill his cup and placate him.

Another shriek rang out.

"What's going on?" the friar roared from beyond the inner door. Sage shot forward, passing through the kitchen to hasten outside. I didn't blame her. The friar would want answers, and while he treated me well enough—I was the only one who could make his favorite meals—Sage often bore the brunt of his rage.

Still, I backed into the corner. Maybe, in his haste, the friar wouldn't see me, and Sage would also get away.

"Sage!" the friar entered the kitchen, to be greeted with another chorus of cries from the outside. Something was happening. Something was wrong.

Another scream from just beyond the door. This time, it sounded like Sage. The friar turned white.

"It's happening," he muttered.

"What?" I pushed away from the corner, grabbing the closest thing I could to use to defend myself—a pot. "What's happening?"

But the friar turned and ran back the way he came, robes flying and sandals flapping.

The door to the outside banged open. But it was only Sage, backing away from the door, her face pale as the moon.

I gulped in a breath as a bearded giant entered the kitchen. He ducked through the doorway and rose up, taller than the tallest man I'd ever seen. Almost twice as tall as any orphan. He loomed over Sage, and then stepped aside, making room for his companion to slip inside. A massive grey wolf.

If this was a nightmare, we were all having it, all at once. My grip tightened on the pot.

"Please," Sage said. "Do not hurt us." She shook but stood her ground.

"No one will hurt them," the warrior said, his voice a gravelly rumble.

"Leave them be," Sage croaked.

The warrior advanced, the wolf stalking forward with him.

Sage glanced at me, and then away. She was so brave, and unwilling to give me up. The warrior had eyes for only her.

I had to help.

I inched from the corner, trying to get closer without attracting attention. More pots sat stacked on a shelf. If I threw the one I held, I could quickly grab another.

The warrior was talking to Sage, who looked as if she might faint. I didn't catch what he said in his deep, growling voice.

"If you leave the others alone, I'll come with you," she answered. Brave, sweet Sage, always trying to save others, at the risk of herself. I wouldn't let her be taken, not without giving her a chance of escape.

I took a deep breath.

The warrior gave up talking and reached for my friend.

I flung the pot as hard as I could.

ULF

Do *you smell that?* My warrior brother, Haakon, nudged me. We stood outside the abbey, waiting amid the ranks of the Berserkers to claim our prize. The woman we'd waited over a hundred years to find.

Our mate.

What do you smell? I asked, using the private link that connected his mind to mine.

A scent like... flowers. Blossoms.

I sniffed the air. The scent was spicy and pungent. But there was a hint of floral sweetness.

There, I pointed to a wing of the great stone building, at the foot of a tall tower. *The scent comes from there.*

But, Haakon nodded to the second half of the building, long and low with a few windows. *The main sleeping area is there. That's where most of the women are.*

I grunted. As we watched, our Berserker brethren broke down the door of the building Haakon pointed at. The warriors rushed in to claim the precious treasure hidden inside.

"We must wait," I told Haakon. "Thorbjorn ordered us to keep watch for any guards."

"There are no guards. These fools don't know what treasure they possess," Haakon snorted. "They do not protect these women. We will take them, and keep them safe."

Glass shattered outward, showering the dark lawn. Warriors leapt out of the dormitory through the windows, now carrying small white bundles in their arms. Spaewives. Women with a magic deep inside, magic that would break the Berserker curse. Some of them screamed, some cried, some cursed and fought. By the end of the night they'd all be claimed as Berserker brides.

"Enough waiting," Haakon hooked his axe into his belt. "Let's go."

Following the floral scent, we ran forward to claim our mate.

LAUREL

The warrior struck down the pot, swatting it as easily as a gnat. I shrank back but he gave me barely a glance before returning his attention to Sage. The wolf barked.

I reached for another pot.

"Leave her alone," I screamed, banging on the pot before I threw it. I grabbed up two more. I was fast running out of things to throw. Not that they did any good.

Sage shook awake and ran back down the hall. Frowning, the bearded warrior stalked after her. I swung a heavy cauldron and let it fly, hoping it'd hit his head.

Instead, it glanced off an axe, clanging to the ground and rolling harmlessly away. Two more warriors entered, crowding the small space.

"Go. I've got this one," the new warrior who'd deflected my missile told the bearded one.

Run, Sage, I thought as the bearded warrior and wolf went after my friend, and turned my back to the wall as two more giant warriors closed in on me.

HAAKON

This is the one. I told Ulf, using the private link between our minds. In the century we'd shared the bond, I'd never felt such a rush of triumph. The beast in my breast howled at the sight of the woman backed into the corner.

"Stay away," the woman growled, as brave as any wolf. She caught up a pan and threw it. I jumped out of the way, and it hit Ulf, who cursed.

"Watch her, Ulf," I laughed. "She's a fighter."

"I mean it," she looked around in desperation, perhaps looking for another thing to throw.

She is our mate, I said silently to Ulf, who confirmed it with a nod. He kept his head turned, hiding his burn scars. Perhaps he didn't want to scare her any more than she was.

Not that she seemed frightened.

She was lovely, with dark hair, flushed cheeks, a bosom that jiggled enticingly. I had to pause and breathe in her scent. Sweet as a mountain blossom, with a touch of spice and smoke. I took a deep breath and caught another, disgusting smell. Cabbage?

"Calm yourself, beautiful. You're coming with us," I told her. "But you have nothing to fear."

Her chest heaved up and down. She wore a little dress, not much, just a thin shift. Did the holy man make her stand there in nothing but her night clothes? Did he like to look at her?

Jealousy gripped me. Ulf felt it, too. No one should look at our mate but us.

I took a step forward.

"Leave me," she said. Her eyes darted around the room, looking for escape. She inched away from me, her bosom straining under the fabric of her shift. Such a nice bosom, two bountiful globes with dusky nipples pressing on the thin cloth. I could easily hold each breast in my hand, cupping their warm weight, soothing and teasing the nipples with my thumbs right before bending down and sucking the peaks into my mouth. Our beautiful mate would writhe and cry in pleasure. She'd try to stop me and I'd pin her arms—

Haakon, Ulf said. *You're distracted.*

"Your home is under attack," I told her bosom. "You cannot stay here. You will come with us and be safe."

"Never," she growled, fierce as a she wolf. She was lovely, our mate. Green eyes, black hair, and a bosom to make angels weep. To make holy men break their vows.

The beast within roared to life. It would not rest until she was marked as mine.

Haakon, you must not lose control.

"Come here," I ordered her.

Instead, she looked to the left, to the giant cauldron sitting on the fire.

"Do not—" I began, but too late. She leapt onto the great

hearth and kicked away the logs supporting the giant pot, yelping as sparks singed her bare feet.

"No," Ulf thundered, as the cauldron tipped and gallons of stinking, steaming liquid gushed over the edge, splashing onto the floor.

LAUREL

I rushed from the hearth, sloshing through cabbage soup. The warriors bellowed in my wake. If I got to the pantry, I could barricade myself in. There was food there, I could eat for days. I could hide.

Strong arms closed around my waist and swung me back.

"Got you," a warrior said. I howled and kicked. Somehow my foot connected with the right place, and the warrior dropped me. I trembled as I backed away. He was fine-looking, with brown hair streaked with gold and tanned skin. Fierce, golden eyes. Strange eyes—like a wolf.

His gaze fell on my breasts, and I cursed the fact that I'd stripped off my dress earlier this night. It was so hot in the kitchens, I liked to wear my shift when I knew I'd be alone.

"Come on, little fighter," the handsome warrior coaxed. "It is not safe for you here. We came to rescue you."

"What?" I half-sobbed. My feet throbbed from the hot broth. I slipped on the soup- covered flagstones and landed half on the hearth. Reaching towards the fire, I thought that if I got close enough, I could grab up a burning stick and rush them—

"Enough," growled a second warrior, pulling me toward him. I froze. He was ugly, a harsh scar marring half his face. I recoiled and he growled again, and caught me in his arms.

"Stop, Ulf, you're scaring her." That came from the handsome one.

Ulf grunted and pushed me forward. "Take her, then, Haakon."

Grinning like he'd won a prize, the handsome warrior Haakon bent so his shoulder hit my middle, and then I was up over his shoulder hanging down his back.

"Stop! What are you—"

"Quiet," a hand clapped on my bottom. I hissed at this outrage, and the hand caressed my right buttock. I almost started shrieking, but a draft hit my face. We were outside.

Muffled sobs and cries came from all around. The moonlight illuminated quite a scene. Large warriors milled about the abbey grounds, some held my friends—the orphans. One giant went by, dragging one of the nuns, who railed and fought him. Sister Juliet—a kind young woman who'd grown up in the orphanage until she took vows. She screamed as he tossed her up over his shoulder and strode into the forest.

"Let me go," I struggled, beating my fists against the warrior's back. My hands might as well have been flowers for all the damage they did to the leather jerkin he wore or the powerful muscles of his back.

He gave a great leap, and landed atop the abbey wall. My stomach flipped and I screamed, but he only crouched and leapt from the wall. Cradling me in his arms, the one named Haakon jogged across the road and plunged into the forest.

Trees blocked my view of the abbey, and just like that, the home I'd known all my life was gone.

ULF

Everywhere I looked, Berserkers carried women out of the abbey. The raid was almost complete.

Thorbjorn? Rolf? I reached out to the leaders of the raid using the pack bonds. Last I'd seen, Thorbjorn was headed down the hall after a little blonde waif, his warrior brother, Rolf, in wolf form by our side.

Ulf? Did you get out? This from Rolf.

We found our flower. I reported. *Haakon has her.*

Good. We scent evil here. Best you take your mate and run.

Happy hunting, Rolf, I said, just as a fierce wind shook the bond. Magic came tearing and snarling to fray the pack links.

I picked up my pace, racing to catch up with Haakon and the woman as a warning echoed down the bond.

The holy man did a spell to call the Corpse King. He is coming. Get out!

LAUREL

In the dark woods, the moonlight lit our path.

"Here we are, love." Haakon crooned as he set me down. He grinned at me as if we'd met in a tavern and he'd wooed me, instead of breaking into a holy sanctuary and carrying me off in the middle of the night.

"Who are you?" I cried. "What is this? Why have you taken me? Why are you here?" I shook, teeth chattering as they did when I was afraid.

He touched a finger to my lips.

"Do not fear," he said gently. "You're safe now. We are here to protect you."

"Then leave us alone," I cried, remembering my frightened friends.

"We cannot. If you stay behind, a great evil will claim you. It is on its way, even now. Without our rescue, you will lose your life."

"What?"

A howl went up, an otherworldly sound. A great wind rushed passed us. I ducked against the warrior, huddling in his shadow.

"What was that?" I shivered in the sudden cold, my shift not enough to keep out the chill.

"The evil that seeks you."

"I don't understand." I couldn't keep from pressing against him.

He rubbed my arms, soothing the goosebumps.

At his touch, my body softened, turning towards his. He towered over me, strapping chest and muscled arms making me feel small and petite, an oak to a shrinking flower. I'd never seen such a powerful warrior. If he told the truth, if I could trust him to protect me, then I need never fear again. I couldn't imagine anything could stand in his way.

The howl went up again, and I let him pull me closer.

"What's your name?" he murmured, his fingers finding the curve of my neck and cupping it, holding me against him.

"Laurel."

"Like the mountain flower."

I nodded, my cheek pressed against his leather jerkin. I tried to push away, and was only able to raise my head. He wouldn't let me go. Something hard probed my belly. I tried hard not to think what it was, and ignored the excitement that thrilled through me.

The warrior smoothed my hair away from my face. "You are mine now, Laurel."

"I don't know what you want with me." I was a good cook, and men of the village called me beautiful, but that was not enough to raid an abbey. Was it?

"It's all right," he said as the wind tossed the trees above us. The wild weather was no normal summer gale. My spine prickled with unease. Yet when he spoke of keeping me safe, I believed him. In the circle of this giant warrior's arms, I was in the calm center of the storm. "You can trust me."

His rough fingers tipped my chin up.

"I—"

My words cut off as his mouth slammed down on mine.

Heat blazed through my body, burning a path from my lips to the apex of my thighs. I clung to his powerful arms, pressing myself into the safety of his body as a storm raged through me.

"What was that?" I gasped when he drew away. The rush of warmth faded a little, leaving an insistent throb between my legs. The ache tightened my nipples, flushed my skin, and left me tingling, alive. I'd never felt this way before.

I wanted to feel it again.

"That," he said with satisfaction, "is why you should trust me."

HAAKON

Our mate's cheeks flushed. Even in the moonlight, I could tell her creamy skin burned. I wanted to kiss her again, and see what other parts of her body would warm.

The enemy is coming, Ulf spoke across our bond. *We cannot hide her much longer. We must go.*

I scooped the woman up in my arms. She squeaked in surprise, but wrapped her arms around my neck.

"Just a little journey, love. Stay quiet."

A wind swept over us, chilling to the bone. Laurel fell silent. Her fingers dug into my shoulders. She smelled sweet under all that burned cabbage.

She wasn't fighting. My kiss had worked like magic, waking her heat.

Behind me, Ulf snorted.

It's true. I told him smugly. *Just scent her arousal.*

All I smell is burnt cabbage. Shaking his head, Ulf picked up his pace. *Stay here. Let me scout the way.*

I crouched in a pool of moonlight, the better to study my

captive. When the wind picked up, she shivered, and I pulled her closer.

"Little love," I murmured and she pressed her lips together. Worry on her face clashed with her enticing scent.

"My name is Haakon," I offered. "You are safe with me. I swear on my axe."

"My friends. The ones you took. What will happen to them?"

"Your friends are safe. We will not harm them."

Her heart thumped wildly. her fright set my beast prowling, ready to taste new prey. I nuzzled her shoulder, stopping when her breath caught.

Haakon, Ulf warned.

Just a little nibble. I turned my head and my lips brushed her ear. She leaned against me with a little sigh. *She is ready. She is almost in heat.*

Not now, brother. We must take her to safety.

A strong gust shook the trees.

Laurel whimpered.

"Hush," I told her. "You are safe now with us."

"I don't even know you," she said, even as she relaxed in my arms.

I nuzzled her hair again. "And yet, we would die for you."

The wind rose again, a plaintive keening that set my hair on end.

"What was that?" Laurel whispered when it died away.

"The Corpse King seeks you. He would take you and the rest of the spaewives as his brides. But you need not fear. Ulf and I will keep you safe."

Something isn't right, brother. Ulf stalked out of the trees nearby. As he came into view, Laurel stiffened in fear. I covered her mouth just before she screamed.

ULF

Pain struck my heart as the woman recoiled from me. I quickly turned the scarred side of my face away.

"It's all right," Haakon told her. "It's only Ulf, my warrior brother. He will not harm you."

"The Corpse King's forces are coming up the road," I reported.

"How did they get here so quickly?"

"I don't know. I can't reach the Alphas, or the pack." My head ached from trying. "There's magic in the air. I do not have a good feeling about this."

"We must get our mate to safety."

I grunted in reply, and started picking a path through the forest. Haakon followed, arms full of the woman he'd chosen.

We've both chosen her, he corrected.

I picked up my pace. *The farther we are from the abbey, the safer we'll be. If we can avoid the Corpse King's notice, then we can head towards the mountain the pack calls home.*

There we will tell the Alpha's we have found our mate.

There are many Berserkers who need mates.

They found their own women at the abbey. This one is ours, Haakon said.

Again, the pain in my heart. I had resigned myself to never taking a mate. To have the chance to claim one—the small hope hurt worse than none.

Unless you don't like her?

I like her well enough. I guarded my own thoughts, lest my warrior brother know my reluctance. Better to never take a mate than have her cringe from me for the rest of my days.

She is round and warm and will be pleasing in the long winter.

If she does not try to bathe us in cabbage broth.

We can punish her if she does. Haakon's eager tone would've made me laugh, if the world around us wasn't turning darker, as if the Corpse King's magic leached away all the light of the moon. *You scented her from the first. You want her. Admit it.*

Very well. I sighed. *This one is ours.* I would keep my distance, and let Haakon claim her. Perhaps it would be enough to satisfy the curse.

Good, Haakon said smugly before adding with more seriousness, *Let us fly to safety.*

As one, we put on a burst of speed. Few things can outrun a Berserker, and we put several leagues between us and the abbey, even weaving around bushes and trees. Gusts of wind tore at the treetops above us violently, raining down leaves and branches.

Our mate cried out. Immediately we both slowed.

"We can't go on," Haakon shouted over the blustering storm. *We cannot outrun the wind.*

We need to find shelter, I agreed.

Who is this mage, that he can control the weather?

We have taken something from him, someone he prizes above all. The young woman clung to Haakon, dark hair plastered against her pale skin. Her curves under the rain-soaked shift were luminous, lovely as the goddess herself.

Reading my thoughts, Haakon hugged our mate closer. *He will never take her from us.*

This way. I bounded down the path. Branches and leaves rained down, missiles flung by the wind. Haakon and I ran faster, dodging limbs and leaping over fallen trees. Trunks of great oaks creaked, the trees groaning and swaying as if they might come down.

The wind ripped one up and sent it into our path with a great rustling crash. Haakon barely dodged it.

Ulf, get us out of here!

Stones shone ahead. *This way—a road.*

I took one step out of the shelter of the woods, and the wind died immediately. *Haakon, wait.* The road was eerily quiet, as if we'd reached the eye of the storm. *Something is wrong.*

A steady trudging sound reached my ears and I threw myself down.

Grey Men. Hide—quick!

Haakon flung himself to the ground, holding the woman close as a huge horde of the Corpse King's stinking servants marched by.

"Keep quiet," Haakon told the woman, his hand over her mouth to reinforce his order. Her eyes were wide with fear. "Those are the Corpse King's forces, Grey Men raised from the dead and filled with magic to do the mage's bidding. If they find us, they may take you. There are too many to fight."

They marched by the place where we lay, rank upon rank of them, newly raised from the grave. With their pale skin and empty eyes, there was no mistaking them for evil creatures.

The woman hid her face against Haakon's chest.

The Corpse King raised a force quickly.

He uses great magic to fight us. He is desperate.

As soon as the Grey Men passed, the wind picked up.

Quickly. I crawled backwards and Haakon did the same, until we could safely rise and run back the way we came.

Head for the hills. The Grey Men move more easily on the road.

The further away we got from the place we'd seen the Grey Men, the more the storm raged. We fought to climb the wooded hills, crouching in the shelter of great boulders when the winds grew overpowering.

Press on, over the ridge. We can find shelter in a ravine.

When we broke from the forest, the trees no longer protected us from the raging wind. A dark muttering echoed around us, as though the sorcerer spoke through the storm. The wind sliced my skin, my limbs grew heavy. My legs moved slower, as if the fog surrounding us was mud. I put my hands over my ears, and some of my energy returned.

Another spell! I warned Haakon.

Behind me, he bent double, bowed against the oncoming gusts that pushed him like a giant's hand. I grabbed him before he tumbled among the rocks.

Take her, he gasped.

Are you sure? But she was already in my arms, trembling. The howling around us increased as I staggered on, my feet finding rising ground. Boulders loomed around us, a giant's graveyard. We'd come to a hilly place, exposed to the sky. No wonder the Corpse King could reach us.

Haakon? I couldn't hear him over the wind. Not even the

brother bond held against the Corpse King's spell. I reached for Haakon, and the pack. Nothing. I was alone.

A thousand bees buzzed in my head, like the witch's magic that made me a Berserker.

I shook my head to clear it.

"What is happening?" the woman in my arms cried.

"Hush," I told her, and gripped her tighter. Lightning lit up the sky, and she screamed. Soft hands pushed at me. Did she see my scarred face, and panic?

Stumbling, I set her down. She scrambled away from me, her shift tearing on the rocks as she ran. Did she not see the cliff's edge?

"No," I bellowed. For a moment, she hesitated, swaying on the rocks. "Come to me." I reached for her. Too late I remembered to clap my hands over my ears to find my Berserker strength. My body moved through air like water.

Laurel backed away, terror on her face. Did the sorcerer's voice torment her, too?

"No—" Haakon dashed forward, blurring past me.

He was too late.

Laurel slipped off the edge of the rock, and fell screaming backwards into the mist.

LAUREL

The howling invaded my head, my body, my heaving lungs, filling me with horror until I drowned.

"Make it stop," I begged, but the wind stole my very breath.

Lightning lit the world and I screamed. The handsome warrior who held me turned into a monster with a scarred face—the left side still firm as a young, rugged man's, the right melted like tallow left too close to a fire.

I clawed at the arms around me, broad and wickedly strong. I broke free, and fought backwards through the wind. And then—

The ground beneath my feet slipped away. The howling stopped. I fell, the wind rushing past me. Night had come, but some evil magic blotted out any moonlight. Someone was screaming, the voice sucked away into the void. My hands clawed at the darkness. Not even the stars would witness my death.

Something struck my body, large and solid as a boulder, but warm. An angel?

A grunt, and the large, black being wrapped itself around me, just as we hit the earth—

Pain. My body rang with the blow, my limbs numb from the cold air and the fall.

Was I dead?

My shocked lungs filled with air. More pain, but a good, alive sort of pain.

I rolled off the soft ground where I'd landed, feeling my arms. My head throbbed, some blood trickled down my bare leg. My shift was torn, dirty, but unscathed. I'd survived.

At the base of the cliff, the air was clear. The moon and stars shone as if they'd never been blotted out. The cliff towered over me, dark and looming as if it might fall and crush everything at its feet. I'd tripped and fallen from the edge, high as an eagle's nest above me.

How was I alive?

A groan shattered the calm. A black shape lay where I'd fallen, a twisted mass on the rocks.

"Oh no." I fell to my knees, nausea washing over me. Someone had caught me midair. Not an angel. A man. I stared at the mangled evidence.

"Oooh," he moaned again. He seemed to be alive. But it was not possible.

I scooted closer to the dying man, scouring my memory for his name.

"Haakon?"

"Oh love," he groaned, his breathing labored. "Next time we dance, let's do it far from the edge of a cliff."

I let out a little sob.

"You all right?" he asked.

My body throbbed as if I'd been beaten, but nothing seemed broken, or even bloody. Unlike him. "I'm... alive. But you—we fell. How..." The sheer rock face glared down on both of us. "How did we survive?"

"Caught you," he rasped. "Broke your fall."

"Oh no," my hands fluttered over his body without finding a safe place to land. The warrior lay twisted on the stony ground, thick, dark liquid seeping out from under his broken form. Blood. So much blood. I could not fix this.

"I'm sorry," I gasped. "I—panicked."

"Not your fault. The wind—"

"It's gone now." The otherworldly howling had fallen silent. The night sky looked normal, the air fresh as a light rain fell.

"Safe now," Haakon caught my hand and gripped it with surprising strength. Warmth surged through me at his touch. I blinked back tears, on my knees, mourning this man I barely knew.

A finger brushed wet away from my cheek? "Why so sad, lass?"

"You're hurt," I choked out. I couldn't bring myself to tell him he was dying. "It's my fault. I ran—"

"Of course you did. We haven't had the best of introductions." A crooked smile flashed onto his face, in between grimaces of pain.

My laugh broke the wall of tension in my chest. The broken man before me had to be crazy, jesting at a time like this.

"Do not worry," he said. "I'll be alright. Berserkers have survived worse."

A mad man, then. I scooted closer and wiped some of the blood on his face with the edge of my shift.

"If injuring myself brings such care, I would've run off a cliff sooner," he joked through bloody lips.

"Shh. Don't talk now. Save your strength." It was a

miracle that he even could speak. I kept my eyes on his face instead of his twisted body.

He stayed silent as my fingers and the rainwater smoothed away the bloodstain, but turned his head once to kiss my fingers playfully. I choked back a broken laugh. Who was this warrior who joked in the face of death and great pain? Our fight in the abbey seemed ages ago, and somehow, I couldn't bring myself to hate him.

When the blood was mostly gone from his face, I sat back.

"Thank you, lass."

"I wish I could do more."

I winced as a cough racked his body, his face contorted in pain. The end would be soon. I should say a prayer. The clouds parted and the moon came out, I gasped.

Was it a trick of the light, or had the cuts on his face closed?

"Haakon!"

I jumped at the shout from above.

"Here's help," Haakon said. "Be calm."

A second later, the scarred warrior came down, scaling the cliff, finding foot and hand holds on the slick rock with only moonlight as his guide. Many feet from the ground, he tensed and flung himself back. I bit back a shriek, but he landed agilely on his feet and strode to our side.

Haakon's body was still twisted, but the gash on his head had healed. I stared and he winked at me.

"What are you?" I breathed.

"Your saviors," Ulf's grim voice made me scramble out of his way. He knelt at Haakon's side. They look at each other in silence, as if communicating silently.

I wrapped my arms around myself, shivering more from worry than cold.

Ulf looked back at me. "Come, lass. You may as well fix what you've broken."

I stared at him as Haakon laughed, coughed, and said, "She doesn't know what you mean, brother."

The scarred face held no sympathy for me. "Both of Haakon's legs are broken. Probably his back as well. Where does it hurt?" The last question was for Haakon.

"Everywhere," Haakon grinned and grimaced at the same time.

"Try not to move. We need to straighten your legs before they heal crooked." Ulf rose and stalked around the prone warrior, taking inventory. Blood stained the rocky ground around Haakon. His jerkin was ripped and torn and damp with blood. At one place, the skin gave way to a flash of white that might have been bone.

Clutching my stomach, I edged away.

"No," Ulf snarled at me, and I froze like a rabbit faced with a wolf.

Haakon grabbed his comrade's arm. "Do not frighten her."

Ulf pulled out a knife and cut away Haakon's bloody jerkin. In a few seconds, the leather lay in shreds around Haakon's brutally broken body.

Cursing, Ulf put a hand against Haakon's side. "Brace yourself," he said gruffly. "I must push the rib back."

A ragged pause, and Haakon nodded, then roared as Ulf pressed the protruding bone back into place.

When it was done, Haakon panted, face white with pain. The rib no longer stuck out, but his chest looked like meat. My hands covered my face, but I peered through my fingers, unable to look away.

"Don't just stand there," Ulf snapped at me. "Help me."

I took a step back.

"You did this to him, damn you—"

"Ulf. No. She is our mate," Haakon gripped his friend's hand, and let if fall, too weak to do more.

"What can I do?" I squeaked. It was my fault this man was in so much pain. On the cliff I wanted blindly to escape, but if I knew what the cost would be, I would've bided my time.

"We must set his leg," Ulf rose to crouch further down Haakon's body. He touched Haakon's knee and the suffering warrior grimaced. "We should wait until your back has healed. But then we will have to rebreak the bones that knit together wrong. Can you feel your feet?"

"Aye," Haakon closed his eyes. "Just do it."

"All right." Ulf stripped off his own jerkin and repositioned himself at Haakon's knee. "Cry out all you want. No need to brave."

Haakon replied with a string of curses comparing the scarred warrior to a castrated rabbit.

His bravery called me to his side.

"I need to snap the leg back into place," Ulf told me. "otherwise it will heal this way."

I nodded.

"Are you going to faint?" Ulf's harsh voice matched the look on his scarred face.

I shook my head. "I'll pretend it's a butcher's cut."

Ulf's brows went up, but Haakon laughed, a pained, rattling sound. "Good lass. You're braver than most. Besides, I already feel like a piece of meat."

"All right," Ulf knelt down, placing his bloody hands on the leg. "Let's get this over with. Grasp his ankle, girl."

"Laurel," I corrected. "My name is Laurel."

Haakon wheezed again, an almost laugh. "She speaks her mind."

"I would rather she obeyed."

"I'm not very good at obeying, I'm afraid." My wild feel-ings unleashed my tongue. "If you wanted a docile girl, you should've left me in the kitchen, and carried off someone else."

ULF

The woman glared down at me. Something flickered in her scent, anger mixed with something intriguing. It was almost enough to take my thoughts off the stink of blood.

Almost.

I turned my head, trying very hard not to think when the beast within me raised its head, smelling fresh meat.

Not meat. I told it.

It's all right, brother. Set my bone quickly and leave me to heal while you hunt. I'll be hungry enough to eat a boar. Even in my mind, his voice was strained with agony. *Our new mate can cook it.*

"Kneel here," I ordered Laurel, directing her to a place at Haakon's feet. She obeyed immediately, spots of color on her pale cheeks betraying her roiling emotions.

I wanted to blister her bottom, but not as much as I wanted to build a giant tower to keep her safe from all harm. Perhaps I would spank her to tears, then hold her and tell her it would be all right.

You should spank her, Haakon panted. *I want to watch.*

Later, brother, I promised, and nodded to Laurel, who had hold of Haakon's ankle. "Keep it straight. On my word. One, two—" I jerked the leg before Haakon could tense.

"Argh," Haakon cried. "Oh, you rotted bastard—" curses trickled from his lips, a colorful description of how I could stick my cock up my own ass. I let him froth while I checked his leg. The limb was still shattered, the skin torn, but at least it was straight.

"It's over, brother," I told him.

Laurel rose, wiping blood onto her shift. She needed a new garment.

She blanched. "Is he going to live?"

"My brother is strong. He will survive," I said fiercely. It was the truth. Not much can kill a Berserker. But maim or scar—that was a different matter. My own face stood testament to that.

I waited for her nod before guiding her to walk back.

I thirst, brother, Haakon said. I unhooked my waterskin and handed it to Laurel.

"Your nursemaid," I said aloud, and prodded Laurel forward.

"And such a pretty one," Haakon rasped. "As long as she doesn't feed me cabbage."

"I wouldn't feed anyone cabbage stew," she said, still standing clutching the waterskin.

"No? Then why make so much?" I couldn't stop myself from asking.

"The friar hated the smell. It made him leave me alone." Her eyes gripped the ground as she spoke.

My hands curled to fists.

"Did the friar bother you often?" Haakon asked.

"Not if I had meat or other food to tempt him. The

cabbage helped keep him away. My friends were not all so lucky."

An animal snarl broke from my lips. Laurel startled and skittered closer to Haakon.

Easy, brother, Haakon cautioned.

I must kill this friar.

If any of our brothers found the man who harmed our brides, then he is already dead. If not, we will return and leave his body for the rats. Haakon tried to prop himself up on his arms, and groaned.

Snatching the waterskin from Laurel's hand, I knelt beside Haakon and bade him drink. "You must rest. I'll make sure our enemies do not come near." As soon as he was done drinking, I backed away again, the beast clawing at my mind. The smell of fresh blood hung in the air, but instead of filling me with human compassion, it only made me hungry.

Haakon watched me go with golden eyes. He knew the danger, the Berserker madness that haunted us, made us less than men. It was not safe for me to stay while my warrior brother was so weak.

But it might not be safe for me to leave.

Ulf, if the enemy comes—

I will do all I can to be sure they do not find us. Even if I must use myself as bait.

I am better bait, brother. You should take her and leave me—

"Never. I will not leave you. Laurel can watch over you. It's her fault you are here." I sounded angrier than I meant. It wasn't the woman's fault she feared us. Women often ran from me.

We will teach her not to fear, Haakon said. *One day she will run toward us, and not away. We will teach her.*

When you are well, I agreed, and turned to go.

"Wait," the woman called.

LAUREL

The scarred warrior pivoted on his foot to face me. I flinched away from his sharp golden gaze.

"How do I care for him?"

The broken man wheezed behind us. Any other man would be dead from his wounds, and me along with him.

"Keep him comfortable. As much as you can." Ulf unhooked a small pouch from his belt. "Here. There's dried meat in there."

"I don't know if he should eat—"

"Not for him. For you. Eat and drink if you must, to keep up your strength." His gaze swept over me, dismissive, even when it lingered on my neckline. I wrapped my arms around my shivering body. My wet shift was near translucent.

With a curse, Ulf handed me a second pouch. "Here's flint. Build a fire. A small one. I will return once I know this place is secure from our enemies. But then I must hunt and get good bloody meat for Haakon." His own stomach growled, and I took a step back.

He caught my arm. That same power I felt in Haakon's

touch sizzled through me, settled into the cradle of my hips. My body leaned into him before I could stop it.

"Do I have your word you will not run?" he asked.

I stared up at him. He angled his head so the unmarred side of his face filled my vision. The dark brows and granite jaw were almost handsome.

I had to lick my lips to answer. "If I did, I would not survive long in this wilderness."

"Promise me you will not," he ordered.

I did not promise. I had to escape. "Where would I go? I am an orphan girl. I have never even left the abbey overnight. I do not think I will survive."

His face softened a touch. "We will take care of you. Watch over him. I will return soon."

"Tell me one thing," I called again before he could disappear in the darkness. "My friends, the others—did they get out safely?"

"I do not know. I cannot reach the pack. I'm sure some did."

I gulped.

"Best focus on our own fate." He nodded to Haakon. "See to him, little fighter."

"But—" I started, and fell silent when Ulf took my shoulders and turned me to face the suffering warrior. Was it my eyes, or did his bloodied chest fall more shallowly?

When I looked back, Ulf was gone.

"Come here, love," Haakon coughed. For all I knew it was a dying man's request, so I went closer and knelt. He reached for me and I caught his arm.

"None of your grabbing me," I scolded. "You must not move. It will disturb your wounds." Wounds that seemed to be closing before my very eyes, his giant body transforming and reknitting itself. He still looked very bad. I swallowed and held his hand as gently as I could.

"Do you wish for more water?"

"No," he squeezed my hand. "Just sit with me, please."

I crouched near him, keeping my eyes on his face so I didn't have to look at the disaster that was his body. "Forgive me," I said again. "I never meant to cause you such harm."

"It was an accident," he rasped. Sweat beaded on his brow. I lay my hand over it.

"You're burning up." My stomach roiled. If fever had already set in, death was sure to follow. "I wish I knew what herbs could help you." My sister orphans knew more of the healing arts, whereas I only knew how to make a nourishing meal.

"Not a fever. It's the healing power."

I watched in awe as a giant wound that yawned on his leg slowly closed, becoming a great shiny weal. "What are you?" I breathed.

"Dangerous," he said. "No one you'd want to meet on a dark night. Unless you are my true mate," he raised a brow at me, as if expecting me to challenge him.

I lay his hand down but did not leave his side.

"Why did you come to the abbey?"

"You saw those forces, the soldiers."

"The Grey guards." I shuddered. My friend Hazel had spoken of them before. She thought the friar had hired them to watch the abbey. The creatures I'd seen on the road looked less like men, and more like the walking dead.

"Grey Men, yes. You felt that wind?"

I nodded.

"That was a curse."

"Why would someone try to curse you?"

"It was aimed at you."

"Me? Why? I'm an orphan. I have nothing."

"It's not what you have, lass," Haakon coughed. "but what you are."

I chewed my lip, wanting to ask more. The warrior's face knotted in pain as he coughed again. I waited until the spasm passed to smooth back his thick hair and wet his lips with water. He let me fuss over him, almost smiling when I leaned over him and my bosoms hung in front of his face. I didn't protest. Anything to help this hurting man. I ignored the warm excitement that filled me.

Haakon drew a deep breath. "Your friend Hazel sent us to rescue you."

"Hazel?" I sat up straight. "You know Hazel?"

"I have seen her. She lives safe among the pack with her mate. She told us of the abbey."

"I thought she was dead. I thought the friar had killed her," I whispered. My heart still twisted, remembering my grief at my friend's disappearance. Could she really be alive —and safe among the warriors? Would this warrior lie to me? "Why did she not come? Or send word?"

"It was not safe. There was no time. We came right away to rescue you. We could not risk the friar alerting his master."

"His master? He serves God."

"Not anymore. He did a spell to call his lord, the Corpse King."

"Why do you call him that? The Corpse King."

"The manner of his magic. Even the dead obey him. They are his servants."

I shuddered. "Necromancy is evil."

"The Corpse King is evil. And he will not rest until he enslaves as many of you and your friends as he can."

"Why us?"

"You are special, little love." His hand caught mine again, gripped it tight.

"How?"

"You are of a race of women whose magic runs deep."

I drew back, but couldn't free my hand. "I am not a witch. I'm a good girl."

"Not a witch. Their magic is tainted. You are pure."

"I don't understand."

"You will."

He coughed, and this time blood bubbled at the corner of his mouth. I ripped the edge of my hem and wet it, wiping at the corner of his mouth. "You must be quiet and heal."

He turned his head and nipped at my hand. An arrow of heat shot through me, flushing my cheeks, dipping between my breasts and warming my nethers.

To hide my reaction, I turned away and sighed. "I suppose you are not used to taking orders."

"Please—do not leave me."

"I will not. But you must drink and rest."

I held the waterskin to his lips and he raised his head to drink before laying back with a gasp and a sigh. Sweat beaded on his brow and I wiped it away.

"Good thing we have you," he croaked, "otherwise it would be up to Ulf to nurse me. He's more likely to toss me off another cliff."

I winced at the jest. "I am so sorry."

"Don't trouble yourself about it, lass. I'll be all right," he stroked my arm. I should be comforting him, not the other way around.

"Ulf will bring meat, and the magic will heal me."

"You should not eat meat. I can make broth, if I have a pot. Cooking was my duty in the abbey."

"As long as you don't feed me cabbage. Ulf will get you

what you need, along with a new garment. Something more sturdy, though I would prefer one as fine and see through as this one." He winked at me.

I pressed my lips together.

"Did I offend you, lass?"

"It's not seemly for you to comment on my state of dress." I tugged my shift as far down over my legs at it would go, but it still left my ankles and a good portion of my calves bare.

"Seemly?" he smirked. "Is it seemly for us to break into your home? Steal you away in the middle of the night?"

"Well, no, but I wasn't going to speak of it."

"Is it unseemly to speak of your kidnapping to your own kidnappers?"

"You are laughing at me," I sniffed.

"That I am. Oh come on, lass. The worst has already happened. Why not laugh?"

"You have an odd sense of humor."

He started to answer and stiffened, agony flashing across his face.

"Haakon? What's happening?" I scooted closer.

"'Tis nothing. Only the healing," his voice was breathless.

"Is there something I can do?"

"Just be with me, lass. That is enough."

I wrung my hands, wishing I could give him something for the pain. The spasm passed and slowly the warrior relaxed. I cast about for something to say, a subject that would not lead to a discussion about my kidnapping or the possibility of Haakon's death.

"How did you and Ulf come to travel together?"

"We are bonded. The magic does it. We share thoughts, feelings, ideas."

What would it be like, sharing my heart's thoughts with another? With a man? I blushed, and Haakon grimaced.

"It's not like that, lass. We bonded together to search for a woman," he emphasized. "One who could free us from the curse. When we find her we will claim her—together." The intensity in his voice made me blush. I wanted to put my hands over my face to hide my cheeks. Two men, together?

"I should build a fire," I started to get up, and Haakon caught me.

"Please. Stay. You warm me better than any flame."

His touch did the same to me, but I didn't mention that. Instead, I settled next to him. When I put my hand over his, he relaxed.

"I'll stay here, if you will rest."

"I will rest if you tell me a tale."

"What tale? I don't know many." The stories told by the nuns were meant to warn us of the consequences of sin. Somehow I didn't think this warrior was concerned with living a chaste and godly life.

"Tell me about yourself."

"Me? There is not much interesting about me."

"I do not agree." His dark gaze made my insides quiver.

"I have lived all my life in the abbey. I never knew my family."

"What do you like to do?" he prompted when I fell silent.

"I work in the kitchen."

"Cooking cabbage."

"Not only cabbage," I smiled. "I bake bread, make honey cakes, broths—"

"Meat?"

"When it is to be had. The nuns and orphans rarely get such fine food."

"Do you like meat?" Haakon's eyes were bright, I hoped with interest, and not with fever.

"I do."

"When my warrior brother returns, he will go on the hunt for us. We will feed you meat every day," he promised.

"What do you like best to eat?" I asked.

"Boar."

"Mmm," my mouth watered. I closed my eyes and tried to remember the mouthful of roasted boar I'd snuck before serving the platter to the friar and his guests. "I would spit the meat—or have your warrior brother do it. Cook it slowly, perhaps with some apple wood on the fire to add to the flavor."

"Go on, lass," Haakon said reverently. I relaxed. A man who enjoyed food couldn't be too much of a monster.

"If Ulf finds apple wood, he may also find early apples. I can slice them with sugar and spices, make a pudding. Or forage for wild onions, leeks, and garlic, and roast them too—"

"Leave the leeks to the rabbits. I wish to hear more about the meat." At my raised eyebrow, he added, "Please."

Stifling a laugh, I went on. "Speaking of rabbit, if Ulf brings back a few of those, I can make a stew..."

THE MOON WAS high and my throat was hoarse from speaking before Haakon's breathing evened out.

Biting my lip, I rose, wincing at the pins and needles in my foot. The rest of my body was stiff and sore, but I would not complain. Not when a great warrior lay on the ground, suffering for saving my life.

If someone had told me earlier today that I would play

nursemaid to a warrior who dragged me from my home, I would have screamed and fainted. But in the cool night air, my head was clear. I owed a debt to Haakon, and would pay it, but once I was sure he would live, I would escape.

Now he lay with sweat beaded on his forehead and a pallor to his skin I didn't like. The worst of the cuts had healed, leaving not even a scar, but the greater injuries were unseen.

He needed more water, preferably broth.

What if he woke and Ulf had not returned? I only had a little dried meat. I nibbled on one strip as I searched for a smooth rock with a small hollow. When I found one boulder, I used the water to wipe it clean. I could soak some of the dried venison and soften it for Haakon. I would need more water.

When I rose from the rock, a shadow fell over me and I gasped.

"Quiet," came Ulf's harsh whisper. "Do not wake him."

I pressed a hand my chest, where my heart fluttered wildly. This warrior's large, powerful body, his rough voice, his ruined face, it all intimidated me. But he wasn't as horrifying as I thought the first time I saw him.

"How long has my warrior brother been sleeping?"

"Not long. He remained awake, I think, to watch over me."

Now Ulf's golden eyes rested on me. "What were you doing up?"

"This," I showed him the rock and explained my plan to soften meat for him.

Ulf shook his head. "I will go hunt now, and feed the choicest bits to him. Eat the rest of the meat. It is for you."

"I do not want it," I said as my stomach growled.

Ulf's hands closed on my arms. I quailed under his direct gaze. "Don't lie to me, little one."

"I am hungry," I admitted. "But I do not know if I can eat much."

His tone was stern, but there was a startling gentleness in his touch. "You must eat, Laurel. Our enemies are about, and when Haakon heals, we'll have a long journey ahead of us. You must stay strong. Do not make his sacrifice for naught."

When I took the meat and tore it with my teeth, Ulf released me and stalked to his brother's side, gliding along like a living shadow. He wouldn't have need of a bow and arrow to hunt, if he moved so quietly. Goosebumps rose all over my body as it reacted to the presence of a predator.

I shivered. Haakon might not be a threat to me, but Ulf could easily force me to his will.

I had to discover what these men wanted with me.

No. No need for that, I chastened myself. I had to escape.

"He looks feverish." Ulf beckoned to me.

"He said it was the healing magic." I wrung my hands, wishing I was not so useless. I did not know what herbs could break a fever. My orphan sisters would, but for all I knew they were scattered to the four winds, captives of more of these warriors.

Haakon coughed, and we both turned. Red spittle dotted the side of his mouth, but he did not wake. I knelt beside him and used a scrap of cloth I'd torn from my shift to wipe it away. When I laid a gentle hand on his forehead, the suffering warrior stilled under my touch. Rigid muscles relaxed.

When I turned back to Ulf, he was watching me, not quite a frown on his face.

"He's burning up. He needs water," I said.

Ulf did not move, and I swallowed my annoyance. I would not be afraid of this man. "Very well." I gathered my shift and rose. "I'll fetch it myself."

He caught my arm before I could walk past him. "You will not run from us. There is no sense in trying to escape." My throat was too dry to answer. I stared into his golden eyes, so beautiful in the harsh, scarred face.

He seemed to realize he'd bared his ruined cheek to me and averted his face. "There is a stream close by. I will walk you to it."

As he guided me through the brush, he kept me on his unmarred side. He'd been a handsome man, before the scars.

When we were walking back, his hand still clamped on my arm, Ulf spoke again.

"I muddied our trail so the Corpse King will send his forces searching the wrong way. I'll leave soon to hunt, and won't return until I have a kill." His hands dipped to my waist to lift me over a wet patch of ground. Again, heat flared to life inside me. I pressed my lips together to keep from gasping. The way these warriors affected me was starting to disturb me. I certainly wasn't going to let them know how I felt.

They hadn't yet noticed. At least, I didn't think so.

Ulf's face was unreadable as a stone wall. "You did not build a fire. Do you not know how?"

"Haakon preferred I stay by his side. He wanted me to tell him stories."

"Stories?"

"I told him of the food I would make for him. I can make a broth, but you must get me some things." I rattled off the list I'd thought of, catching my breath when he adjusted his grip on my arm, making my body pulse with excitement.

"I can get those things. Most of them. I do not know what tarragon is."

"An herb," I said. "You may be able to find it—"

"I do not know herbs." He cut me off in a tone that told me he didn't care to learn.

"I only wish to be sure the broth tastes good," I snapped and pushed away from the frowning warrior. I enjoyed a moment of freedom until the leafy ground gave way to gravel and my foot slipped. Ulf caught me before I fell.

"You all right?"

Pressed against him, my curves molded to his muscles too well. I gave a stiff nod, cheeks heating. I refused to look at him, and he let me go.

"Take more care." Was it me, or did his voice sound bitter? "As for the broth, we've choked down everything but rotted meat. This will be a fresh kill. You needn't worry about the taste."

"I might be able to find something in the woods to use," I muttered.

He grabbed my hand, gripping tightly. "If you think you're allowed to leave and roam about the forest, you are mistaken."

I glared. "Very well."

Ulf stared at me for a beat before his lips twitched. Then he jerked his chin. "Haakon's awake."

The fallen warrior was alert but pale.

"Still alive, brother?" Haakon asked.

"That's what I was going to ask you. How did your nurse-maid fare?"

Haakon grinned at me as I scrambled over the rocks to get to his side. "She is pretty but cruel. Did she tell you how she tortured me with tales of good meat?"

"She did. Soon that will not be just a story."

Haakon drank very, very slowly. I held the skin to his lips and gave him breaks, wetting the cloth and laying it over his forehead.

"Thank you, lass," Haakon said, and I hushed him.

"Thank me by saving your strength and getting well."

He did as I bid, a half smile on his face.

Meanwhile, Ulf stacked kindling in a pile and quickly built a fire. The flames cast a mottled light over his marred face.

I gasped. I knew how he'd gotten his scars.

Ulf shot me a look and I pressed a hand to my mouth.

"It was a fire," he said as if reading my thoughts. "My enemies tried to trap me in a burning lodge. Haakon pulled me out."

"Not much kills a Berserker," Haakon added. "But whatever the healer used to heal his skin made him scar."

Ulf turned away with a growl.

"He doesn't like to talk about it," Haakon told me in a low voice. "I would avoid the subject, and take care whenever you build a fire."

"I shall," I promised. I wouldn't dream of bringing up the subject of Ulf's face. Not only did it seem to bother him, but it was dreadfully rude.

Haakon drank all the contents of one waterskin, I rose to get the second, but had to pass close to Ulf to get it.

When he rose suddenly, I startled.

"Do I frighten you?" he said in a harsh tone.

"No," I said carefully. "No more than he does." I nodded to Haakon.

"You are frightened?" Haakon asked as I knelt beside him with the fresh waterskin. "That's not what I scent in you."

"Of course I am frightened. You kidnapped me."

"Saved you," Haakon corrected.

"Yes, well, I didn't know I needed saving." I wiped the invalid's brow, wondering if he was stronger than he looked.

"And now?"

I sat back on my haunches. Something about Haakon's helpless state made me honest. "I do not know who is more dangerous. You or the ones you say are after me."

"We are both dangerous, little love," Haakon said, taking the cloth from me. His knuckles brushed the side of my bosom and I jumped. His touch woke tingles in my skin and a sudden awareness in my body. "Dangerous in different ways. But you can trust us."

I made myself nod stiffly, even though my body wanted to lean into him, soothed by his crooning tone. I had to keep my wits about me. I had to survive.

Haakon raised a brow. "You clung to me tightly enough when I kissed you."

Pressing my lips together, I shook my head. I didn't need to think about that kiss. My first. A man's lips claiming mine.

And such a man! Even lying bloodied on the ground, he was a sight to behold. Arms corded with muscle, his legs like tree trunks.

I leaned over him to wash away some rusty streaks on his left arm and he caught me in a grip strong as a healthy man's.

"You smell sweet, like a flower. Like a mountain laurel." He brought my fingers to his lips.

"I'm sure it's not proper to speak so."

He barked a laugh. "Proper? Is that what they taught you in the abbey?"

"Yes, to be kind and sweet, and always obey." I tossed my hair, chin jutting up haughtily, all the while pressing my legs together. I felt very hot and strange. There was a trickling wetness between my thighs, but I had just finished my courses. Surely they weren't upon me again.

"Do you always obey? You did not in the kitchen."

I hesitated. Lying was a sin, and the warriors didn't seem to like it. "I do not often obey."

"We will have to train you then, little love. Although, being naughty can be very delicious indeed."

I was about to inform him how it wasn't proper to speak of that, either, when Ulf cleared his throat behind us.

HAAKON

*Y*ou're *supposed to be healing, brother. Not tricking our mate into bed.* Ulf sounded disapproving, but he raised his head to sniff the air, his eyes sparked gold. The woman's warm, floral scent rose in waves, stronger with every passing moment. Her bosom filled my vision. Pale and heaving. She blinked rapidly, her plump lips slightly parted.

Her heat is almost upon her, I reported. *She responds to us.*

Enough, Haakon. You must rest.

Spoiling my fun already? But he was right. I needed to sleep, though I did not look forward to it. The magic curled around my bones, knitting them together in the most efficient, if painful, way. My dreams would be of torment. I'd rather stay awake, with the raven-haired vision before me. Even in a torn and dirty shift, my little nursemaid inspired the most delightful stirrings in my—

"Laurel," Ulf interrupted again. "I'm leaving on the hunt. Can I trust you with my brother?"

"Yes," she raised her chin. "You did so before."

"I want your word."

"I want him to live." Her voice softened as she turned to me. "You saved my life. I owe you and will repay the debt."

"An orphan with a sense of honor?" Ulf raised his brow. Laurel didn't appreciate his mocking.

"More than I can say of you, barging in to steal me away in the middle of the night," she snapped, and flushed when she realized how she had challenged her captors. Before she could cringe, I caught her wrist.

"Did not still your tongue," I grinned. "I like it."

"I'll fetch more water before I go," Ulf said. *She should not abandon you now.*

Was there a chance she would?

She looks longingly at the forest.

She's looks with more longing on me. I stretched gingerly, spreading my legs a little. It hurt, but Laurel's blush when her eyes fell at the apex of my legs was worth it.

So you say, Ulf returned and flung the waterskins down, narrowly missing my head. Too late I remembered he was sensitive about his scars.

She looks at you, too, brother, I told him too late. He'd already strode off, disappearing into the forest, leaving me with the pale, sweet miss.

"Are we safe here?" she blurted out.

"Safe enough. Ulf will see we remain so." I forced a smile to my lips. I hated being so weak.

Laurel shivered and tucked her knees to her chest. It was the darkest part of the night, and even the fire couldn't keep the terror of the darkness away.

"Come to me, lass," I breathed, reaching for her. She shrank from me before she remembered herself. "I won't hurt you."

"You are ill. You cannot hurt me."

Even with a broken back, I could still overpower her, but I didn't mention it.

"Lie here," I patted the ground at my side.

She bit her lip, looking tired and miserable.

"I offer my warmth and nothing more. I won't take anything you don't want to give."

With a jerky nod, she moved to settle close by. She lay stiff at my side.

With a groan, I slid my arm around her shoulders.

"Haakon, no, you should not—"

"Hush." I squeezed her to my side. After a bit she relaxed.

"Sleep, little one. It's been a trying night."

"I don't think I can," she whispered. I tightened my hold, wishing I could roll atop her and lick and suck her curves and secret places, wearing her out with pleasure. She'd sleep then, and have good dreams. As if she could read my thoughts, her scent, which had mellowed, grew pungent again. She shivered, but her face was flushed. When she tried to pull away, I caught her close.

"What's wrong, lass?"

"I do not feel well," she muttered.

"Have you felt this way before?"

"No," came her soft answer. Her legs moved restlessly, but I didn't let her go. "I'm sure it'll pass."

My fingers slipped from her arm to the curve of her chest. As I stroked the smooth skin of her arm, she sucked in a breath but didn't stop me.

"You enjoy laying here with me."

"No," she huffed.

"You are lying, little love. Do not try deceive me." I said firmly, then lowered my voice. "Now tell me, what do you feel?"

Her voice came very small. "I don't know."

"You are hungry for your mates."

"No," she protested, and I moved my hand up to collar her neck.

"Another lie. I warned you, little love. Speak false again, and you will be punished."

Her pulse jumped under my fingers, but the air filled with her sweet scent.

"You are not afraid of me. You are afraid of how you feel."

"You don't understand," she whispered. "I'm a good girl. I should not feel such things."

I clasped her chin and brushed a thumb over her lips.

"You are our mate. You respond as you should." My hand slid down her chest, tracing the pale hills of her cleavage.

"I don't know what's happening to me." Her voice was so broken, I stopped my teasing fingers.

"Calm yourself, little love. You have nothing to fear. We took you from the abbey for this purpose. You will serve as our mate, and we will cherish you always."

A little whimper escaped her throat, but she clung to me.

"Soon you will understand." I stroked her hair until her body melted into mine, her breathing growing even as she slipped into her dreams.

Wishing I could hold her properly, I followed her into sleep. It had been a century since I'd held a woman safely in my arms. I looked forward to a new day with my blushing, virginal mate and her honeyed scent.

But when I woke, she was gone.

LAUREL

A pang of guilt pained my heart as I crept from Haakon's side. He lay in heavy slumber, barely twitching when a butterfly wafted over his face and landed on his knee. The daylight lined his peaceful face, and the ravaged lines of his body. He was healing, but the angry weals and broken skin told me he would spend this day, at least, prone and still healing.

An ordinary man would be dead.

I should stay and nurse him, and keep my promise. But his touch in the darkest hours of the night woke feelings I could not control, feelings best left in slumber.

So I left one waterskin and took the other, and slipped away.

I found the path Ulf had lead me on in the dark. Had it been only one night? I was still tired, my body aching from the fall.

My legs burned after a few steps. I'd lived my life in the shelter of the abbey, rarely straying beyond its walls. At times my errands sent me to the village to buy a special meat or spice, but since I'd grown into a woman, I found others to go in my place. Men stared at my curvy body as if I were a piece of meat they wished to buy. I was happy to stay in the kitchen, slaving over the hot pots and oven, only leaving to pick an herb or gather the harvest.

How had I come to be here, stumbling through a forest, guilt gnawing me for leaving my captor and my savior lying at the foot of the cliff.

Brambles tore at my ragged shift, and I tugged the garment close to my body. I might as well be naked for all the protection the thin fabric gave me.

No wonder Haakon looked at me with such hunger.

And yet, he was gentle. He both shocked and soothed me, and seemed to want nothing more than to stand between me and my fear. One night, and I could not imagine leaving him. Or Ulf—as stern as he was, careful to keep the scarred side of his face turned away so as not to scare me. Could I survive without their protection? If the Corpse King really was out there, ready to harm me, was it wise to run from the warriors' protection?

The more I thought, the more my steps dragged.

I'm safer on my own than with them. They make me... feel things.

I reached the stream and knelt to fill the waterskin. When I raised my head, a giant wolf stared at me from the thick brush. I froze like a rabbit, wide eyed and trembling, unable to move or breathe.

The predator slunk towards me with gleaming eyes. It held a few limp furry bodies in its jaw. It had already caught its dinner, a parcel of rabbits.

Perhaps it wouldn't want me.

Still holding my gaze, it bent its head and lay down its kill.

The air shimmered. A gust of wind rose with the thick,

open smell like the air after a heavy rain. The wolf... Changed. In its place rose a man, naked with a pelt over his shoulders.

I shrieked and ran back the way I came.

ULF

L aurel crashed through the bush, her white calves flashing under her shift. Even frightened, she gave off a rich perfume that called to the beast. It would gladly chase her for miles, but I grabbed her before she did herself harm.

"Naughty one. What did I tell you about roaming through the forest?"

She stilled as she recognized my voice. I turned her so she could see the contempt on my face. Too late I realized she would have a clear view of my scars, but she didn't wince at their ugliness in the harsh light of day.

"What did I tell you?" I shook her, fear making me angry. Another hour, she might have strayed out of our protection. I knew she would run. I was waiting for it. I just hoped she would've waited until she was stronger, and the threat of our enemies no more.

Without waiting for an answer, I tossed her over my shoulder and strode back to camp.

Haakon was waiting for me, awake, his hands crossed behind his head as if he'd simply laid down for a moment.

The tenseness in his jaw told me the magic was doing its healing work, and he was suffering.

"Look what I found in the woods," I let Laurel down and she backed away.

I'd left my clothes and weapons in the woods and gone hunting as a wolf. The Change left me naked but for a pelt over my shoulders. She seemed more afraid of my naked-ness than anything else. Silly girl.

"What a lovely catch," Haakon said out loud. Using our bond, he added, *I'd hoped for fresh meat, but once I am well fed, I wouldn't mind eating her. No doubt she has the most delicate flavor.*

I barked a laugh, and Laurel jumped. Taking a rope, I bound her wrists and looped a section around her neck, then led her like a pet to Haakon.

"Keep her close," I ordered, handing him the leash.

"It's all right, little love," I heard Haakon soothing her as I walked away. "He will not remain angry for long."

I went back to the stream and gathered up the waterskin and rabbits. Back at camp I built up the fire, skinned and spitted the game, letting the tension build.

I didn't think you were cruel, Ulf.

I am not being cruel by making her wait. I merely wish to be calm when I punish our mate.

I wasn't speaking of making her wait. No doubt she's happy to delay her discipline. I meant me. Haakon mock pouted. *I want to see you punish her. I am an invalid, I have so few plea-sures left to me.*

I had to bite my cheek to hide a smile.

Truly, Ulf, she is contrite enough.

Laurel sat with her head bowed. Even when I took the pelt from my shoulders and draped it over her knees, she barely raised her head.

"For you," I said. "To keep you warm. I'll get you new garments when I next leave. This time I thought it best not to be long gone on the hunt. It is good I was not, because by the time I would've returned, you might've been lost. Or fallen into a ravine. Or captured by the Corpse King's servants—and who knows what evil would befall you then?" I tore a hand through my hair, heart constricted with fear— the likes of which I hadn't felt for a century. "Do you know that we rescued Hazel from a cave filled with bones? Whatever the Corpse King's purpose with the spaewives, none of them survive. You are alive because of us." My voice rang over the rocks. Laurel sat hunched with the pelt gripped in her hands, crying.

"Oh, lass," Haakon soothed. *Enough, Ulf.*

"I am sorry," Laurel sobbed. "I didn't want to leave. But I must. I cannot remain here."

Crouching, I gripped her knee through the pelt. Her pale skin flushed with the first signs of the feverish heat that marked her as a spaewife and made her a perfect Berserker mate. I wanted to comfort her with sweet words like my warrior brother, but my voice came out harsh as ever.

"You can run, but we will never let you go. You belong to us, now."

LAUREL

Ulf left me to my tears. Haakon held the rope tying my wrists and collaring my neck, but he was gentle and didn't tease me. Every once in awhile, he stiffened and sucked in a breath. His body went rigid, sweat beading on his forehead. At those times I might easily break free of my leash, but shame kept me kneeling beside the suffering warrior.

Truly, I was a wicked girl. Compassion was one thing, but how did I come to care for such dangerous men? What was wrong with me?

"Are you frightened of Ulf, lass?" he asked when the worst of his suffering had passed. "He will not punish you, too much."

I bit my lip. "He... he was a wolf."

"Ah, yes. That is one of our forms," Haakon said simply, as if that explained the extraordinary. "But even when we are the wolf, you have nothing to fear."

"So you can turn into a wolf too?"

"Yes. Big, dark, and hairy." He waggled his brows. "The ladies love it."

I was too shocked to laugh at his joke. "Is that part of the curse?"

"Yes. A part that is more of a gift."

A shadow fell over me. I cringed, but Ulf ignored me.

"Here," Ulf offered Haakon a skewer of meat and held it as the wounded warrior ate slowly.

I sat up in protest. "That is almost raw." The bloody meat turned my stomach. Ulf glanced at me but said nothing.

"It's good," Haakon mumbled between bites.

When Ulf stalked back to the fire, I followed as much as the rope would allow.

"He needs broth. Healing soups. I can make them."

"We are not in a kitchen."

"Can't you fetch a pot from the village, when you get me a new gown?"

"Best we not camp here too long."

"You can't move him. Not yet." Perhaps not ever. I gulped down my doubts, but Ulf seemed to sense them.

"He will heal," he said, his face dark.

"He will heal faster if I cook soups." I was being ridiculous, but I did not care. Better to bluster and argue than think on how I really felt.

Ulf grunted. He freed my hands to eat, and he pressed a skewer of meat upon me before feeding the rest to Haakon.

"Eat, little one," Haakon urged when he noticed me sitting with the skewer in my hands. At least my portion of the rabbit was well cooked.

Haakon and I filled our bellies, but Ulf ate not a bite.

"Can you move your legs?" Ulf asked when Haakon had wiped the last of the grease from his face and drunk almost a skin of water.

Haakon nodded.

"Show me." Ulf stood over the wounded warrior,

watching closely as Haakon did a series of exercises that left beads of sweat on his forehead.

Ulf crouched to wipe his brow. "I may need to splint your back."

Breathless from exertion, Haakon shook his head.

"If it heals wrong, we'll have to rebreak it."

"I know," Haakon gasped.

"Can you Change?"

"Not yet. I am—" Haakon bit off the rest of that sentence.

Ulf lay a hand on his shoulder. "Rest. You will be well. If I have to call a witch—"

"No. No witches."

"Very well. Here is your nurse, then."

Ulf tugged my collar and leash. I sat up and tried to smile at my pale patient.

"So pretty," Haakon didn't miss the chance to charm me. "the sight of her is enough to heal me."

Ulf snorted. His good nature faded when he turned to me.

"I'm leaving to patrol. I will return soon. If you run again, I will tie you so you cannot move. And your punishment will be double. Tell me you understand."

"I understand," I whispered. Only when the scarred warrior left, I dared to breathe.

I huddled near Haakon and spread cool cloths on his brow. Fever burned again, tinging his cheeks red. A spasm went through him, then another, shaking his legs and leaving him limp.

I stroked back his hair, peering at his glassy eyes until he blinked.

"Does it hurt very much?"

"Better with you here."

I bit my lip again, bowing my head. Haakon grasped my wrist. "What is it, lass?"

"I should not be here."

"Why not? You are safe with us."

I shook my head vaguely.

"Did a man hurt you?" his tone turned so dark I whipped my head around.

"No. I didn't often venture outside of the abbey, and certainly didn't stray among men. I was a good girl."

"You are good," He stroked my thigh. Again the heat twisted through my core, body awakening, a flower turning to the sun.

I sucked in a breath, seized with the need to run again. As if he sensed it, he used the leash to tug me closer.

"You are ashamed."

"When you touch me, I feel... strange."

"Does it feel good?"

I looked away. I couldn't lie, but I couldn't tell the truth.

"Where is the fighter who challenged us in the kitchen?" His hand cupped my face, shaking a little with exertion. I clasped it, holding it up as he stroked the apple of my cheek.

"You do not run from us. You ran from yourself." With that pronouncement, he sagged, and I lowered his arm.

"I am not supposed to feel this way." I kept my eyes on the ground.

"No more running. We will help you face your fears. We will keep you safe."

"You make me feel things," I whispered as his fingers played over my thighs. "It would be better if you'd left me in the kitchens."

"You wish to hide? You wish to lock all your beauty away? Look at me, Laurel." He waited until I met his gold gaze. "You must embrace who you are."

"It's not right."

"It is."

I shook my head. "That is not what they taught us."

"Then we will teach you anew. But not right now. Right now, I wish to lie next to a beautiful woman and nap the day away." He pulled the leash until I lay down beside him.

We dozed together in the sunlight, me tucked against the warrior's side. Even though I had slept little last night, the rest I had gotten had been deep and peaceful. As troubled as these warriors made my mind, my body was at ease. A bud tightly furled, longing for more. The warriors held the secret to coaxing such a bud to open. Not harsh words or angry blows, but gentle sunshine and delicious rain. Soon, my body would bloom. I would give myself to them, and they would not even need to touch me.

I woke with a start as Ulf entered the clearing, carrying a large cauldron that sloshed as if filled with water. The warrior's corded muscles flexed as he set it down gently near the fire.

"Your pot, milady," he said. "And—" from a makeshift pack, he produced a lady's gown, a bright scarlet brocade that rolled in thick folds to the ground. My breath caught. I had crossed to him to touch the brilliant fabric before I knew what I was doing.

"Bright as a robin's breast," Haakon murmured. "The Corpse King won't need to scry to find her. She'll stand out in all but a field of poppies."

"The Corpse King can scent her, as we can. The shade of her gown matters not," Ulf told him, and turned to me. "We will not let him near you. I thought the color would suit your pale skin and dark hair. And your lips, bright as berries."

"I—" I licked my lips, looking from Ulf to the dress. "Thank you."

But when I reached for it he held it away.

"Not so fast. You still must be punished."

I gulped.

"If we were in the lodge," Ulf continued. "I would've stripped you from the first, and made you earn your clothes back. You would not run far if you were naked."

Haakon chuckled.

Ulf lay the gown over a clean rock. "But I don't want you catching a chill. You will wear your shift, and you will use this water to bathe Haakon." He nodded to the pot.

My hands twisted in my thin garment. "Bathe him?"

"Come on lass. Am I so frightening?" Haakon grinned. His pain seemed to fade whenever he teased me.

I shook my head. The warrior's large, battered body would look better cleaned of blood. "But," I turned back to Ulf. "What about his breeches?"

The scarred warrior handed me a knife with a large, wicked blade.

"Oh no," Haakon spoke up. "Whose punishment is this? You leave me at the mercy of a lady and a long knife?"

"She can shave you, too," Ulf called over his shoulder as he swaggered off, his axe cocked on his shoulder.

"I'm jesting, lass. I trust you."

I swallowed hard. I did not trust myself.

"It's all right, Laurel. Hand it over." Haakon used the blade to cut his breeches away. I helped remove the rags, taking care to ease the cloth away gently so as not to disturb his position. I left his loincloth, but when I leaned over him, my hair draped over his middle and he sucked in a breath. I stilled. "Did I hurt you?"

"It's nothing of consequence," he gritted out. "I know something that will make it feel better."

"What?"

"If you wash me naked." He winked.

"I will do no such thing," I gasped, even as heat curled through me, a wicked excitement that made my loins ache.

"Come lass," he picked up a cloth and tossed it to me. "This is your punishment." Then he lay back, grinning as his body drew my eye. He was so broad and strong, clad only in a loincloth, tented with his hard length. A few inches and he'd be bare to me...

"Laurel," Haakon called me from my reverie. I blushed, and he laughed. "Do you need more instruction on how to wash me?"

"I-I don't know if I can do this." In his presence, my body came alive. I knew some of my orphan sisters suffered a fever that left them moaning with lust. They kept it a secret, in case the nuns found out and punished them. If I touched Haakon as I wished, my desire wouldn't be secret anymore.

"Please, lass. You promised to care for me." Haakon made his voice contrite, but I wasn't fooled.

"You must behave," I told him.

The wicked glint in his eye told me he would do no such thing.

In a huff, I wet the rags, and bent to my work. The grime and blood cleared away from the smooth skin with satisfying speed. I rubbed gently up and down the long lines of his muscles, so firm under my fingertips.

I couldn't keep myself from smoothing my hands over the scars on his pebbled abdomen.

"I got those before I was a Berserker," Haakon said.

"When was that?"

"Many, many years ago. In a land to the north, across the

sea. Countless kings have come and gone since I was young."

"Truly?" I was shocked. For all his scars and strapping muscles, Haakon didn't look older than a young man from my village.

"The magic keeps us young."

"What magic could do this?" I breathed, and a shadow fell over his face.

"None good."

His sadness was so unlike Haakon, I kept caring for him, cleaning his muscles until they gleamed, dabbing gently around his wounds. I even threaded a cloth between his toes.

"That feels good," he sighed, and I propped his foot in my lap, rubbing the sole, hoping he would soon relax and return to joking. The silence weighing over us did not feel good.

"It was a contest," he spoke abruptly. I kept quietly massaging his feet. "There was a jarl who would be king. He called for a competition to decide his best warriors. I was young, but I was strong and fast. My father had trained me to fight with axe and sword. I competed with all the jarl's men, and rose quickly through the ranks."

"Was Ulf there?" I asked.

"Aye. He fought alongside me. In the end, there were only a hundred of us out of a great force. The jarl split us into five groups, twenty men each, and sent us to the witch. I—"

My fingers faltered as Haakon's voice did.

"I don't remember much beyond that," he rasped.

"It's all right." I took up his other foot and continued massaging him, even working up his legs, soothing his taut calves.

"The magic makes us strong. It does all but keep us sane. Over the years, it eats at our mind, until we go mad."

"Mad?"

"Aye, lass. There is but one cure. We must find a mate."

I pursed my lips. They'd made it clear they thought I was their mate.

"Laurel."

I raised my head. Haakon stared at me with shining eyes. Magic-born and fey. And yet still a man. I couldn't ignore the stiff pole tenting his loincloth now. The size of it made my throat dry.

"I know we stole you, and you were afraid. I wish it could've been different. You must believe me."

I nodded.

"You don't know how much you mean to us."

Suddenly, I couldn't bear to look at him. Bowing my head so my hair curtained my face, I squeezed his leg, and dropped a kiss on his knee.

"So sweet. Our little flower."

"I, um, have finished washing you." I sat back on my haunches. My shift was wet and see through, but I didn't try to cover myself. It was part of my punishment, and Haakon's look of awed pleasure made my insides tighten in delicious anticipation. Not that I enjoyed his attention, I scolded myself. I simply preferred happy Haakon to the haunted warrior who told me how he came to be cursed.

"There is one more part yet to wash," he said, and moved his loincloth aside.

Heat suffused my neck and face. His manhood jutted out from his body.

"I-I don't think—"

"You are a lovely lass. Look what you do to me."

"Does it hurt?"

His laugh rippled the muscles in his chest. "It aches. It needs your healing touch."

I didn't know what to say. I'd heard of how men were shaped, and seen stud bulls at the market. One of the village men my age had bared himself to me, and laughed with his friends at my blushes. I'd scurried off, and found reasons to stay away from the village after that. Even though the lad hadn't touched me, I felt ashamed.

I did not feel ashamed now. I should, but I did not.

"Hand me the cloth, Laurel," Haakon said, and when I did, he wrapped it around himself, squeezing and tugging a little before flinging the rag away. His large hand slid up and down the now slick length, working it in a way that brought a grin to his face. He never took his eyes off me.

I realized I shouldn't be watching. "Um—" My hand fluttered over my face.

"Look if you like," Haakon spoke through gritted teeth. "Soon you will learn to do this."

"I will not," I gasped.

"No? Even now you look like you wish to touch me."

"I... simply wish to make you feel good... No," I said hurriedly. "Not like that. I just want you to be well."

"This will make me feel very, very good," he said. I watched mesmerized as he worked himself. I knew how it could be between a man and woman, but how could such a large thing fit inside me?

"One day, you will wake me with your sweet mouth on my cock. I'll tell you to lick every inch, and you'll obey like the good girl you are. And when I am done," his words tumbled out faster. "You'll swallow all my cream."

Something was happening. Haakon's hips jerked, he grunted, and whitish fluid poured from the tip of his cock, over his hand. He cursed over and over.

I leaned forward. "Haakon, are you hurt?"

"No, sweetness. Get the cloth." When I did, he nodded to his still hard member. "Clean it." My hands trembled as I leaned over him.

"One day, you will lick it all up," Haakon whispered. "Ulf and I will fill you and leave you painted with our seed, so that any man can smell it and know you belong to us."

My cheeks were so hot they must have caught fire, but I wet the cloth again, and wiped away all the thick cum. He beckoned me close and swirled a wet finger over my chest, then let me clean his hands.

When Ulf returned, his eyes flared like torches. Tipping his head back, he sniffed the air.

"I see you've been busy."

"I have," Haakon said, satisfied. "And our mate has earned her reward."

"Oh?" Ulf looked from Haakon to where I sat, face flushed and arms wrapped around my legs to keep from trembling, though I could not keep my cunny from throbbing.

"Oh yes."

"I did nothing," I spoke up. "I only washed him."

"And watched as I pleasured myself. Should I ask you next time what you learned?"

"No. I... no."

Haakon laughed. "Don't worry. I won't force you to do it. One day, you'll beg me."

Shaking my head, I glared at him.

"Enough teasing," Ulf said. "Laurel, come here."

"What now?" I muttered, though I scrambled to my feet. Haakon liked to joke, but Ulf was so stern and serious, I dare not disobey.

"It's time for your first punishment."

"But, I already did my punishment."

"You think washing me was punishment? You are cruel," Haakon pretended to pout.

I rolled my eyes. Ulf drew me to him until I stood between his legs.

"I told you we would make you mind."

"I'm being good," I protested.

He raised a brow.

"I am trying," I amended.

"You are doing well. But we are in danger, and expect perfect obedience. Our lives are at stake."

I nodded.

"You were punished in the abbey?"

"Yes." I gnawed my lip. "How will you punish me?"

"However we see fit. This time I will take you across my lap, raise your skirts, and spank you until your skin is red."

I gulped. "Must you?"

"Yes. We are your masters now and you will do as we say. Running away deserves a swift, severe punishment."

"You are everything to us. We will keep you safe," Haakon added in a gentler tone, but Ulf looked at me sternly. "Tell me you understand."

"I understand."

"Shift off," he tugged at the garment. There was no room for argument in his tone. My mind on my punishment, I drew the shift over my head. He tossed it away and I crossed my arms over my chest, hunching a little.

"Are you going to make me remain naked?"

"No. But you must undress to bathe," he murmured.

I sucked in a breath. The chance to wash sounded lovely. The water in the pot would be nice and warm now.

"Would that I could bathe you, as you did me," Haakon called.

"First your spanking," Ulf drew me over his knees. I clutched at his legs as he tipped me further, until my bare bottom waved in the air. "Put your hands on the ground." Quivering, I did as he asked.

To my surprise, the pain didn't start right away. His large hand cupped my bottom, rough fingers tracing my curves.

I shifted. "Please."

"Hush," he ordered. "I am preparing you for your discipline. It would not do to bruise this lovely skin." His hand swept up my leg and I almost cried out. Slick juices gathered at my apex, threatening to run down my legs.

"Do you wish me to punish you?"

I wanted to get it over with before he could see what was happening to me. "Yes."

"Ask me."

My stomach flipped with humiliation. "Please, Sir, punish me."

A rare chuckle from Ulf warmed me through. "As you wish."

His hand spanked me, small, sharp swats at first that built in intensity until the cracks rang out across the clearing. I clung to his leg, hair over my face. Warm pressure built at my core, threatening to spill out of me.

"No." I wrenched up. "Stop. You must stop."

"Laurel?" Haakon struggled to sit up. "What's wrong?"

My backside was red and throbbing, but that wasn't the cause of my distress. I backed away from Ulf, my hands over my bottom. "You can't punish me anymore."

"Laurel, stop." Fury flashed in Ulf's face, and I dared not take another step. "Lie back down over my knee, or I'll pick a switch next."

"Please," I sobbed, but did as he commanded.

"Good girl," he said, and something in me melted further. I cried harder.

He rubbed my bottom, even dipping his hand between my thighs. I didn't fight. They were too big and strong, and I was too wanton.

A few more smacks and he had me back on my feet, staring at me with an almost worried expression.

"Well, Laurel, did you learn your lesson?"

"Yes," I cried. He caught my wrist.

"Do not rub. I'll tie your hands," he warned.

I nodded frantically, and he let me go.

"Come here, lass." Haakon opened his arms. Forgetting that he was hurt, I flung myself down next to him, sobbing into his chest.

"Ulf only punished you because he was afraid you would run again. 'Tis not safe. You must know that."

"I know," I wailed. But it was not safe for me to stay, either. The men had awoken another beast—one inside me. If I didn't get away soon, I'd never be free.

ULF

The sobs of the woman filled the clearing. I frowned.

I took care not to hurt her. I barely spanked her.

It wasn't you. She suffers because of her fears.

Remembering myself, I turned from the touching scene. Haakon could soothe our mate. I only frightened her. I should've kept to my vow, and never agreed to take a mate. Laurel deserved another, even if the thought made me sick.

Uncurling my hand from a fist, I caught a whiff of sweet musk.

"Well, that's interesting," I murmured.

"What?"

I lifted my hand coated with Laurel's juices. Even across the clearing, the scent was clear.

Haakon's eyes glittered. "Very interesting."

I busied myself with chores until the woman calmed down. Once she no longer sniffled, Haakon sent her to bathe her face and hair. It killed me, but I pretended to ignore the splashing and soft sighs of our mate as she enjoyed the water I'd warmed for her.

You can watch, you know. She's your mate as much as she is mine. The heat in Haakon's voice told me he'd enjoyed the whole show.

Next time.

Once we have her in our lodge, we should keep her naked.

I couldn't think ahead to a home with a mate. There was still so much danger. The Corpse King hadn't found us yet, but if Haakon didn't heal quickly, it was only a matter of time.

When Laurel stepped out of the bath, I was waiting for her. Steeling myself, I raised a new shift, woven from the softest linen and hemmed with beautiful needlework. Laurel's wide eyes told me she'd never seen such a fine garment.

I motioned her close but turned her. "Bend down," I murmured, and added when she sucked in a breath. "I only wish to check your bottom." Her pale curves bore a lingering redness. I cupped a generous handful and massaged it, soothing her when she rocked from side to side nervously. There were a few raw lines from where my fingers had caught her sit spots. I grew hard as iron knowing my hand had made the marks.

At last I drew her upright. Her face was as red as her bottom.

"The beast within us longs for a mate to cherish, but also to discipline."

"Please," she whispered. "I'll be good."

"You are a good girl," I praised her. "But we also will not hesitate to take you in hand, to teach you our ways. But after punishment, comes reward."

I helped her dress into the shift, and then the red gown. The fabric flowed like wine around her legs. She looked like a queen with her long, dark hair braided into a crown.

"It's so beautiful," she breathed.

"Our mate will always be clothed in finery."

"Unless she is at home alone with us," Haakon corrected. "Then she must always be naked."

Laurel rolled her eyes. A soft smile suffused her features. She looked at the ground before me, almost... shy.

"Will you thank Ulf for fetching you such a fine gown?" Haakon prodded. I glared at him.

Before I knew it, Laurel had curtseyed. "Thank you, Sir." She came close and took my hand and kissed it. I stilled as her lips touched my rough knuckles, the beast inside me roaring to life.

She must have known the danger, for she trembled a little when she raised her eyes to mine. "I don't deserve it."

I just stared at her. She gazed unflinchingly on my ruined face.

"Of course you do, lass," Haakon called. "Our mate deserves the best."

A stubborn look came over her face, one that told me she did not accept that she was our mate.

"You're welcome for the dress," I told her. "Suits you better than a dirty shift."

She bobbed her head again, and I cursed myself for insulting her old clothes. I almost drew away, but she kept hold of my hand.

"Wait," she examined my grimy palm. "Do you want me to wash you?" Her cheeks were bright as robin's breast, but her scent told me she didn't loathe the idea.

As much as I wanted to say yes, I couldn't bear to see her face when she touched my scars.

"No need, lass. I don't need a nursemaid. I'm whole." Cursing myself again for insulting my warrior brother, I snarled and strode away.

NIGHT HAD FALLEN before I returned, a giant stag draped over my shoulders. The beast raved inside me, even after a long hunt and a few lonely sessions with my cock in hand. A fire now burned inside me. Only Laurel could put it out. So, after running the perimeter to check for signs of the enemy, I carried my game to camp.

The light flickering through the trees gave me pause, but I schooled my steps and ignored my old fear.

Haakon dozed, his arm propped under his head, as if he'd laid down for only a moment. It did me good to see him sleeping peacefully. A brush with his mind told me his pain was fading.

The woman sat near the blaze, poking it with a stick. She'd cut her old shift into an apron to protect her fine dress. A few dark hairs had fallen out of her braid, but other than that she looked as regal as ever. Her beauty almost made my heart stop.

"Ulf?" she looked worried. I must look a monster with the massive prey over my shoulders. More monster than usual.

"For you," I told her and shrugged the buck down. The ground shook where it fell.

"What am I to do with that?" She gawked at the giant body. Tip to tip, the antlers stood as tall as her.

"Cook it." I knelt and split the chest cavity with my claws. Too late I remembered I should hide the beast from our woman. She averted her eyes as I carried the buck's heart to Haakon.

"Here, brother."

Thank you. Haakon said, not wasting breath to speak before he tore into the raw meat. *If you didn't return soon enough, she threatened to feed me onions.*

I chuckled and strode back to the fire, licking blood from my fingers. Laurel sat with her hands folded in her lap. Sure enough, there were a few wild onions cooking in the embers. *At least it wasn't cabbage.*

Once Haakon finished the heart, I gave him a few more organs and ate my own share of the offal. Blood smeared the prone warrior's body. As he ripped into the liver, Laurel made a distressed sound.

"Don't worry, lass," Haakon said between chews. "You can always wash me again."

Scoffing, she turned away, crossing her arms over her chest. Gone was the meek thing I'd left with a reddened bum. In her place was the fighter with the queenly mien I remembered from the kitchens. I raised a brow at Haakon, who shrugged.

Using saplings that I'd cut earlier with my axe, I built a giant structure to spit the meat. Before I went on the hunt, I'd stripped off my clothes so I could Change at will. The magic left me a loincloth about my hips, but otherwise my body was bare. The fire that ruined my face left a few scars on my arm and side, but nothing too ugly. Unlike my face.

Once the buck was cooking, I washed in the stream, returning with my clothes in hand. Several times I glanced at the woman, daring her to look at me. She kept her eyes on the ground, but I knew she noticed. The color in her cheeks matched her dress.

Seating myself close with the good side of my face

turned to her, I took up the stick Laurel had and poked her onions.

"Did you venture far into the forest to find these?" I asked.

"Not far. Haakon could see me the whole time."

I rolled an onion out and regarded its steaming form. "You were worried Haakon would need food before I returned."

"Yes."

Using a few wet leaves, I picked up the steaming onion and peeled it gingerly. "I suppose I will not leash you, then."

"Thank you."

"I will not have to leave again to hunt. You may have lost your last chance to escape."

She didn't reply. I studied her stiff form. Her punishment hadn't softened her. Instead, our mate had put up walls.

"There's plenty of meat, if you'll accept it from my hand."

"Thank you," she said again, as her stomach growled.

She is determined to be polite, I noted to Haakon.

Mmm. She thinks she can control her desires by pretending to be civilized. But they claim her all the same. Haakon grinned. *Can you smell it?*

Raising my head, I sniffed the air. There it was—under the thick scent of roast meat, and onions—a woman in heat.

She is ripe for the plucking, Haakon smacked his lips. Laurel seemed to know we communicated silently, for she glared at him. I noted how she kept her legs pressed together.

I'm surprised she is so calm.

She is not. She is frustrated. The slim fingers gripped her new gown as if her world were tilting, and she tried to hang on. *Feed her, Ulf. Fill her belly. Then perhaps we can convince her to sate her second hunger.*

I tossed the onion on the fire and saw to the buck, slicing into the browning meat. The woman's squeamish look told me she required more cooking time.

"Thank you for looking after my brother," I said.

"I do very little."

"Still, he's healing well."

"You know as well as I, that is the magic, not I." She pursed her lips, as if talking of magic left a bad taste in her mouth.

"You do not like our magic?"

"It makes you very powerful."

I examined my fingers. The blood had washed away easily but my nails were still a bit long. The beast was close to the surface. "It does, until it drives us to madness."

"I think you are already quite mad," she muttered.

"What was that?" I raised a brow, but tonight she had no fear of me.

Anger flashed in her eyes. "You attacked a defenseless abbey. This is civilized country!" Her bosoms heaved.

"We will never be civilized." I sat down beside her, close enough for my bare leg to brush her clothed one. She stiffened again, but after a moment, relaxed closer. Interesting. She resisted until she forgot herself and leaned into me. She didn't seem to know she was doing it.

"When you attacked the abbey, you committed a crime against God."

"We do not worship your gods."

That shut her up. She jerked back, cheeks flushed, mouth open. I'd rise and feed my cock through her plump lips, If I wasn't so sure she'd bite me.

With great reluctance, I stood and paced to the other side of the fire.

Haakon chuckled.

You better heal soon, I told him. Controlling myself was becoming harder with the beast enticed by the heavy musk of a woman in heat.

I closed my eyes and breathed it in. How long had it been since I'd lain with a woman?

"I can't believe I am trapped with such heathens," Laurel muttered under her breath.

"Oh, and you're a right proper miss," I observed. "Cooking in your shift?"

The blush spread over her. "It was hot in the kitchen."

"I wasn't complaining. You're welcome to strip down to your shift anytime you like. Though out here you might catch a chill."

She snorted.

"Don't worry, lass." Haakon said. "I'll keep you warm."

"That won't be necessary."

When she pointed her nose in the air, I couldn't resist goading her. "When we are returned home, Haakon thinks we should keep you always naked. I am considering the idea."

"Surely not!" she gasped.

I gave her a wide grin, showing my teeth.

She fell silent, shrinking in on herself.

Not too harsh. Haakon admonished. *I like it when she speaks her mind.*

Most men would prefer a quieter mate. I couldn't tear my eyes from her as she trotted across the clearing, hips swaying under the gown. The movement made my cock leap in my breeches.

Good thing we are not most men, Haakon chuckled, and winced.

"Come, lass," I said when the meat was done, and I'd carved a pile onto a flat stone we'd use as a plate. "Time to eat."

"I'm not hungry," she said.

"Stubborn," I mouthed to Haakon. Instead of arguing with her, I made short work of the meat and carved another platter, then took a seat where the breeze might waft the juicy scent in her direction. The wind was strong that night, and sure enough, soon after I sat down, her stomach growled loud enough to hear.

"Enough," I told her. "You must remain strong if you are to fight us."

A pause, and she jerked from her seat, and sat down beside me. The beast crowed in triumph, even though I knew she would not sit so close if she wasn't so hungry. She reached for the meat and I tutted. "No, lass. From my hand." I held up a piece of meat.

Closing her eyes, a resigned look on her face, she closed her lips around it.

Red claimed my vision as her hot mouth sucked the juices from my fingers. "Mmmmm," she moaned at the second bite, her head tipped back and face suffused with bliss.

I growled.

"What's wrong?" the woman sat back, licking her lips. My cock tightened painfully. "Did I do something?"

"No, lass. Not your fault." As I shifted in my seat, I caught a small smile on her face. "Take care. You tempt the beast."

"Do I?" She purred. "I only wished to obey."

She leaned in again, her bosom full on display, and I caught the back of her neck and leaned in. I breathed in her scent still sweet and rich as a honeyed fruit, ripe for pluck-ing. "Careful, Laurel," I whispered in her left ear. "You play a dangerous game."

Her legs shifted restlessly. I sat back, the beast in me enjoying the glazed look on her face. But I forgot myself and let the light of the fire illuminate the hideous mass of scars that was my right cheek.

Her breath caught.

"It's all right, love," I quickly angled the right side of my face away. "I know you would never want one who looks like me."

She blinked and drew back, her gaze falling on the ground.

Ulf—Haakon began.

I threw up a hand to silence him. *I don't wish to hear it.* Carving another plate of meat, I set some beside Laurel and took the rest to Haakon.

I was only to make a jest. Between my face and your body, we make one whole man.

It wasn't the same and he knew it. *Soon you will be whole again.*

I disassembled the spit and hung the carcass from a high tree to deter animals from stealing our meat. At least, any animal that dared come close to Berserkers. Drawing aside my loincloth, I marked our territory, spraying an arc around the tree with the game. As soon as Haakon was well we'd be gone from this place. We'd take care in our journey, and with any luck, the Corpse King will have forgotten us.

It wasn't until I was walking back that I caught a whiff of something rotten. The last time I'd smelled it—

"Laurel!" I shouted, racing towards the fire. Cold wind swept through the camp ahead of me, a gust catching the fire and sending flames licking towards our mate.

She screamed, and I reached her side and hoisted her up, pushing her away from the showering sparks. Whirling, I kicked dirt over the fire, but it wasn't enough. The wind whipped the flames to a frenzy.

The woman crouched near Haakon, leaning over him to protect him from the wind.

"What is happening?"

"The Corpse King. He has found us." I ran to the two of them. "Haakon, I must move you."

He nodded stiffly.

"Look out," Laurel cried as a rock came whizzing towards me. I turned and it struck me in the arm.

"Now!" I shouted.

There wasn't time to make a travois. Seizing Haakon under his arms, I dragged him to a small gully, protected by great boulders.

"Laurel," I called and reached for her. She raced and clung to me as we squeezed under a rocky overhang protecting us from the rocks and clumps of dirt rolling down from the cliff. The Corpse King shook the very earth.

A boulder smashed not a foot away from us. Laurel sucked in a breath and hid her face in the crook of my neck. "Why does he do this? Why does he not leave you alone?"

"He wants you." I hugged her as the wind howled above us, and buried my face in her hair. "He cannot have you."

LAUREL

When the storm died, we ventured from our hiding hole. In the ravine, there was little dry ground. Haakon lay in a little crevice in the rocks, cramped and barely able to fit half his body. One calf bled where a rock had struck it. His breath came in short, pained gasps.

Ulf dropped to his knees, tearing strips from his own clothes to make a bandage. "I should not have moved you so soon."

"It's all right, brother."

"No, my fault. I built the fire too large."

"Showing off," Haakon gasped, and I knelt close to shush him. I held his hand tight while Ulf went to retrieve his supplies. Sleep quickly took the wounded warrior, leaving me alone with his scarred companion.

I cursed myself for flinching at his scars. The left side of his face was so endearing, I forgot the whole of the man. Handsome and scarred. Stern, strong, and unyielding as a rock. And yet...

When I shivered, unable to get warm, Ulf slung a wolf

pelt over my shoulders and gathered me into his strong arms. Any game that I'd been playing fell away. I needed him, and could not hide it.

Sometime later, I woke with a start. A body lay next to me, burning like an inferno. A strong body clad only in a loin cloth. For a moment, I thought I'd snuggled next to Haakon, but then the man raised his head, and the moonlight caught his ravaged cheek.

"Ulf."

"I didn't mean to frighten you," he said, angling his face to hide his scars.

I don't know why I did it, but I touched his chin, stilling him. I don't know why he didn't cringe, but he closed his eyes as I traced the line of his scars, smoothing the harsh ridge with my fingertips.

Not all of his skin was mottled and melted. The right side of his face was smooth, even pleasing. His lips were firm and fine.

I shifted uneasily. Liquid trickled from my nethers. I snatched my hand away, rolling to my back. I should be sleeping, resting so I might plot my escape. I should not be thinking about his lips...

"Thank you for saving me," I whispered.

His body jerked beside mine. Shock at my gratitude?

Before I could think, I rolled onto him. I pressed my curves into his hard body, marveling at how we fit.

"Laurel?" his hand touched my hair, hesitant.

"Mmm," I answered, halfway to falling back asleep. I was not playing a game. I didn't know what I was doing, but one thing I did know. Ulf didn't think he was worthy of a woman's touch, love, or affection. I wished I was brave enough to stay and prove him wrong.

But I could not. I had to leave before my feelings bound me to these men forever.

WHEN I WOKE Haakon lay sleeping. He didn't wake when I moved. He looked whole.

Ulf was gone, most likely checking for danger. It was time. Rising, I wrapped the pelt around my shoulders.

My feet squelched on the muddy leaves as I followed the hidden stream out of the ravine. The sun was high, and I was well and truly lost when I realized I was not alone.

Stomach quivering, I faced my tracker.

"How long have you been following me?"

In answer, Ulf walked towards me. His boots made no noise on the gravelly ground. He made no move to hide his ruined face as he took my wrist. I followed willingly, only hesitating when our camp came into sight. Haakon was awake and sitting up.

I'm sorry, I mouthed to him. His gentle gaze was more censure than I could bear.

"Are you going to punish me again?" I asked Ulf. Some part of me had always known I wouldn't escape. Had I run only so they could bring me back?

Ulf drew me into his arms and held me, the harsh lines of his face and stern frown at odds with his gentleness. I shook against him. When he drew away, I kept my eyes on the ground, unable to look at him or Haakon.

Ulf pulled me to face him and tugged at my gown. "Off."

"What?"

"You disobeyed. I'll give it back when I am sure we have trained you not to run."

Slowly, I shrugged off the gown and handed it to him.

"All of it." He draped the dress on a bush and folded his arms. He would not force me or hold me. He made me make the choice to obey on my own.

Once naked, I wrapped my arms around myself.

"It'll be all right, lass," Haakon called.

Ulf bound my wrists and wrapped a leather thong around my neck, taking care the knot would not tighten when he pulled the lead.

"You'll sit with Haakon."

Haakon pulled me to lie on my side next to him.

His hand stroked my arm as Ulf went to work. His axe chopped saplings, and lashed them together to make a frame, much as he had to make a spit for the stag.

"What are you going to do to me?" I whispered.

Haakon cupped my cheek. "We'll make sure you never want to leave."

The sun hung low in the west before he was done making a sturdy frame. Ulf left and returned with plenty of rope, and more rabbits for dinner.

He did the cooking, and brought over a bowl of food.

I raised my hand for him to untie, but Haakon clucked and held a morsel to my mouth. Cheeks burning in shame, I let him feed me like a babe.

"How long will you leave me like this?" I asked.

"As long as it takes you to learn," Ulf said in voice hard as flint.

I winced and bowed my head.

Ulf crouched in front of me.

"Why did you run?"

"I cannot do this," I pleaded. "I cannot be your mate."

Ulf's cheeks tinged red and he looked away.

"You already are." Haakon's hand drifted over my breast, secret pleasure curled through me.

"I was raised to be good a good girl. You should find someone else."

Ulf put his hand on my knee and stroked. His touch was maddening. I winced away and his face turned to stone.

"Please, just punish me."

"Very well," he said harshly, his expression closer to hate than I'd seen it. I'd rejected him, I realized. Last night, I'd held him close, but I'd destroyed any fragile tenderness when I ran. As Ulf untied me and led me to the frame, I wondered if I could atone for what I'd done.

My heart beat faster as he secured my wrists and ankles to the structure. He lashed my legs and arms and middle to the saplings. I found myself spread eagled, legs far apart and cunny exposed. I squeezed my eyes shut and quivered as much as my bonds would allow.

What would he do? Would he whip me? My back was to the frame, but my large breasts were exposed.

I opened my eyes when Ulf cleared his throat. He held a switch. I gulped.

"Do you know this implement of discipline?"

I nodded. The nuns had used it on us, often.

"As I watched you leave, I was tempted to whip you up and down with it. Haakon does not wish to mark you. I must confess I'd like to see you marked by my hand." He gripped my breast, no hesitation at touching my body now. My heart beat faster, breath coming in gasps as he squeezed and massaged my flesh. Helpless, bound before him, I never wanted his touch to end.

My cunny wept.

I sighed when he stepped away.

"I'm going to strike you, as a warning. You'll be getting a spanking later. We will punish you as much as it takes to bind you to our will."

I nodded, unable to look away. His harsh gaze captured me, held me tighter than any rope.

The firelight played along the edge of his ravaged face as Ulf snapped the switch a few times, testing it. I winced at the supple sound.

"Not too many, now." Haakon spoke up.

"Just a few." Ulf said, and flicked the switch across my breasts. I cried out, and a stinging red line appeared across the pale skin. He placed the switch under my breast, lining up his next shot. My chest heaved. The switch left a mark under my breasts.

"One more," he said and rubbed the switch between my legs. I bit my lip to keep from crying out.

"Give me your tears, Laurel. This is how you please your masters. We would risk everything to keep you safe. Our very lives. You will not throw yours away."

My lips trembled. *I'm sorry,* I wanted to cry out but had no words.

He marked the tops of my thighs and biting into my cunny.

I whimpered.

"Enough. See that you don't earn more."

I shook my head frantically.

He turned the frame and I saw what else he had done.

Haakon now lay on his back between two rows of large boulders on either side of him.

"Gently, brother," Haakon instructed. Ulf just grunted as he lifted me, frame and all, and carried me over to Haakon, where he set the sturdy structure over the prone warrior. Haakon's dimple flashed up at me. I hung suspended over him, helpless, held fast in my many bindings.

"What are you doing?" I thrashed but couldn't free myself.

"Whatever I want." Haakon craned his neck to kiss me. His lips seduced me as roaming fingers plucked my nipples, explored my cleft, squeezed my bottom.

A sharp smack made me cry into Haakon's mouth. Ulf stood over us, switch in one hand. The other spanked my other buttock, hard enough to make me yelp.

"Poor little love," Haakon crooned. "Did Ulf mark you? I will make you feel better."

Carefully, he scooted down, and I moaned when I realized his intent. With my body suspended on the frame, my breasts hung down like fruit. Haakon was all too eager to lick and suck them, swirling his tongue along the switch marks to soothe them. He kissed the line of my hurts until I gasped.

"Enjoying yourself, brother?" Ulf asked.

"Not as much as I could be."

"She's responsive." Ulf's finger pressed against my bottom hole.

I yelped and tried to flail, but couldn't budge.

Haakon chuckled. "I want to taste her sweetness." He set his teeth around my nipple and I panted. Turning his head, he nipped me and my hips bucked.

"Please, no. I will go mad."

"You accused us of being mad. Perhaps then you will better match us. Or perhaps the madness was in the abbey. Beautiful, luscious girls all taught their flesh was sinful," Haakon tsked. "We will teach you a new lesson."

Ulf lifted the frame again, turning me around so I hung over Haakon's legs. His giant cock waved in the air, stiff and proud as a flagpole.

"Oh, no," I groaned as I felt Haakon's hot breath on my cunny.

HAAKON

Laurel sounded horrified. Her hips strained in their bounds. "Surely you cannot mean to..."

"Why not?" I nuzzled her lower lips. Turning my head, I rubbed the rough side of my jaw against the tender skin of her inner thighs, just lightly enough that she whimpered. Not in fear. But in need.

It didn't take long for her sweet scent to overpower me. My cock stiff as a stone, I delved my tongue into her folds and lapped up her juices with long swipes of my tongue. Her hips shimmied as if she would escape me, and when I circled her tiny, stiffening pink piece of flesh and sucked on it, she howled.

"I think she likes it," Ulf observed. The bastard probably had his cock out and was toying with her mouth.

Not until she is trained not to bite us.

"Suck on this, sweetling," he crooned, and put his thumb to her mouth. Via the bond, he shared how her cheeks hollowed in her effort to obey.

I busied myself between her thighs, searching for the right pressure to make her come undone. She arched and shook, desperate noises escaping her lips. Her body undulated with her climaxes. The frame was a thing of brilliance, Laurel's beautiful body displayed like a tapestry over the interlacing wood. Her breasts hung down within easy reached. I squeezed them like ripe fruit, and delicious juice poured into my mouth.

I came so hard, I splashed her with my seed. Pain throbbed through my back, but it was worth it. Reaching up, I rubbed the sticky stuff into her belly and breasts. The beast within slept, content now that she wore my scent.

A grunt told me Ulf had finished as well. "Lick it, sweetling." I grew hard again imagining Laurel's sweet flesh painted with cum.

Spreading her lower lips wide, I kissed her, probing her secret places with my tongue. A scream tore from her mouth and her cunny clenched, begging for cock. I cleaned her of all wetness, and slowly started to circle her clit again. A howl built in her and I tongue fucked her mercilessly, not stopping until she cried out and went limp.

Enough, Haakon. She fainted.

The sun flooded my vision as Ulf took the frame away, laying our mate out and checking her pulse.

"Still alive, but I shall cut her down."

"Give her to me." I reached out and waited until Ulf placed her in my arms. I massaged her limbs, paying special care to the red marks where the rope had held her.

She stirred, and I gave her a little water, but for the rest of the evening, into night, she drifted in my arms.

LAUREL

In the morning, I said nothing about the events of yesterday. As for the frame, I didn't even look at it. I worked extra hard on chores as a way to absolve myself, grateful when Ulf allowed me a shift.

Ulf said nothing to me. Midday, he returned from the hunt. We ate quail, and when I'd finish he beckoned to me, drew me over his lap and bared my bottom to his hand.

"How many times am I to be punished?"

"Again and again," he squeezed my bottom. "As many times as we see fit. Unless you've decided not to run from us again. Have you?"

I shut my mouth. I could not stay, and I could not lie.

Ulf spanked me until I was limp. When his hand went between my legs, checking my wetness, I didn't even whimper.

"How is she?" Haakon asked.

"Soaked," Ulf said, and went back to swatting my bum, "You belong with us," his voice murmured in time to the rhythm of his swats. A pressure built in me. I writhed to relive it but it would not go away.

He smacked my bottom again and again. When he went back to touching me, I protested, pushing up. He caught my wrists and held them at the small of my back, and wrapped his heavy leg around mine. I could not escape the beautiful longing in my body. The spanking went on until I felt a rush of pleasure, a release.

"Oh God," I sobbed. "Oh God."

"Hush." Ulf held me as my climax died away. "You did nothing wrong. There is nothing wrong with you."

My bottom throbbed for the rest of the day. After dinner, Ulf threw his bones into the woods and held out his hand once more.

"Again, Laurel."

"No," I said, but didn't fight when he pulled me over his knee.

"You like it."

"I do not," I whispered and shut my eyes as he laid the lightest slaps on my bare backside, just enough to tempt my ardor, stoke the fire into a roaring blaze.

"Do not lie to me. You do."

"I should not then," I cried, kicking my feet. "I don't know why I feel such things."

"And yet you do."

"Good girls do not do such things."

"And yet here you are, a good girl, allowing me to do these things, and enjoying it."

"I do not enjoy it!"

"Oh yes, you do..." The swats grew in strength until I was gasping. My backside burned, but not as much as my cunny. One more blow, and the dam broke, pleasure flooded through me.

It wasn't until Ulf sat me up and wiped my tears away that I realized I'd been crying.

"Good girl," he held me and I cuddled back, feeling strong and safe with this man who would not let me run from myself, or him.

Gently, he set me on my feet. "Go now. Lie next to Haakon and keep him company."

Haakon held open his arms to me. I folded my body next to his, taking care not to disturb him. He seemed stronger every day, but moving him had delayed the healing.

I LAY BESIDE HAAKON, my whole body flushed as if I'd stayed too close to the fire. "I don't know what's happening to me."

"'Tis natural. 'Tis your heat."

"Why am I like this? Why do you want me?"

"Shhh, you're perfect. The beast requires an anchor. Someone to love. Someone to master. Someone to control. A mate."

I licked my lips so I could speak. "You think I'm your mate."

"I know you are. Soon we will bond. You will join with me and Ulf, and our minds will link. We will be as one."

I almost cried out. The emptiness in my body, the longing—I knew now what would sate it.

"Haakon, I cannot. I have nothing. I am nothing. How can I be your mate?"

"When we came to the abbey, we scented you from afar. As soon as we found you, we knew. From the first pot you threw."

"I am afraid."

"You're not afraid of us. You spent so many years squashing who you are. Hiding from the world. Your fighting spirit. Your laughter. Your beauty." He squeezed a handful of my hair, tugged it lightly. "But you can't hide from us. I think that scares you most of all."

"It's the only way I'll be safe."

"We will keep you safe."

I had no answer to that. I wasn't afraid of danger. I was afraid of how these men made me feel. The powerful arousal overwhelmed me until I was lost. When the heat consumed me, would there be anything of me left?

"I don't know," I whispered.

"You don't need to know. You don't need to think any more. You just need to trust us. Trust me."

I craned my neck to see his face. The laughing warrior. He'd leapt off a cliff—for me.

"All right."

He squeezed me, seeming to hold his breath for my answer.

"I trust you."

Catching my chin, he claimed me with a kiss. The fever burned in me. I pushed into his body, desperate to feel his skin against mine.

I broke the kiss. "I don't want to hurt you."

"My body was broken for you. Do what you will."

"I'll kiss the hurt I caused you."

Undoing my braid, I let my hair stream over his skin, and pressed my lips down his hard body. My tongue explored the breadth of his muscles, my hands mapping planes and ridges. I grew lost in the terrain of him.

"Oh lass," he sighed and let me grasp him under his loin cloth.

"I don't want to hurt you," I repeated. I'd caused this man enough pain.

"You won't," he gazed on me with such trust. "Do whatever you like, lass. I'm yours."

Crawling down between his legs, I bared him to me. I lay my breasts on either side of his cock, rubbing him up and down with my soft flesh. Ducking my head, I tasted him.

"Oh lass," he groaned. Smiling, I squeezed my breasts around his staff, alternately kissing and licking the tip. His thighs tensed.

"Come," he pulled me back to lounge beside him. He kissed me as he stroked himself.

"May I?" I wrapped my small hand around him, marveling at the silky heat.

"Lovely lass. Lovely Laurel." He let me work his cock, and ran his hand over my body. His fingers slid between my lower lips, finding the sweet spot and circling it. He teased me until my hips tightened, and I gasped.

"Say my name, little love," his lips found my ear. "Tell me who owns your pleasure."

"Haakon."

"Do you want your pleasure? Tell me."

"Yes."

"Beg your mate."

"Please," I could barely think. "I need it. I need —Haakon—"

"Cum, lass."

As my orgasm sang through me, I pumped Haakon's cock faster. It was hot and hard in my hand.

"Laurel—" Haakon's hips bucked as he came. I let the creamy fluid coat my hand. He trembled a little, sweat standing out on his pale forehead.

"Haakon? Does it hurt?"

"Yes. The pain is worth it."

Fetching a cloth, I cleaned him, and snuggled into his side.

"So, when do we bond?"

"The bond can take some time to form. I think that first, Ulf must accept you as our mate."

"He hates me."

"He does not." Haakon kissed my hair. "Ulf does not think he is handsome enough to deserve you."

"I do not mind his scars. I've come to almost like them. I should tell him."

"You can, lass, but beyond that, you must show him."

A ROUGH HAND WOKE ME.

"Laurel, get up." Ulf handed me my gown and boots. "Dress. Be quick."

I obeyed, sparing only a glance at Ulf. As usual, I couldn't read his expression.

The air was cool and dry, a hint of foulness in the breeze. But above our heads, grey clouds boiled in the sky. In the distance, birds cawed along with a noise like a great many rushing wings.

"Do you hear that?" Ulf asked.

"Yes," Haakon answered.

"The Corpse King's found us. The Grey Men are coming."

"We knew it would come to this," Haakon said quietly.

Ulf jerked a nod. In a swift movement, he rose and lifted his axe.

"What?" I flew up in terror. But Ulf only let the axe bite the ground near Haakon, who took it up.

"Don't worry, Laurel. They will not easily kill me." His eyes flashed.

"What? No," I scrambled to the wounded warrior's side. "Haakon—"

Ulf caught me about my waist. "We have to go, Laurel."

"No," I cried. "I will not leave him!"

"You must," Haakon said. "I cannot keep you safe."

I writhed in Ulf's arms. "At least let me say goodbye," I begged.

He let me down and I flung myself next to the prone warrior.

"Oh lass," he sighed as I lay my head gently on his bare chest. "You must be good. Promise me."

"I promise." I squeezed my eyes shut, hiding my tears. Turing my head, I pressed a kiss to his heart. He caught my chin, tipped it up and claimed my mouth. As always, my body responded, the beautiful surge of emotion. Why had I ever fought this?

"Now, you must go."

"I don't want to."

"Do as Ulf says. If you don't, I'm afraid you might lose your life."

"I'll obey."

"Good mate." He kissed my forehead.

"We must go. Now," Ulf ordered, pulling me to my feet.

I hastened behind him, trying to keep up. I risked a glance behind me. Haakon sat upright, propped against a boulder. He looked nonchalant, but I knew he was helpless.

I felt like screaming. Would I ever see him again?

When I stumbled, Ulf swung me up into his arms without comment.

The forest blurred as the warrior ran. I felt a moment of shock when he slowed.

"Wait here." He set me down and disappeared. I crouched behind a boulder. The numbness inside matched the eerie silence of the forest.

Ulf returned to my side within the minute, and picked

me up before running a different direction. But within a few minutes, he skidded to a halt and cursed under his breath.

"What is it?" I clung to him, I could not help it.

"Grey Men. I scent them ahead."

Ulf changed direction again, only to stop again. "We're surrounded. There are too many of them to fight."

If I craned my neck, I could see what he scented. Rank upon rank of Grey Men, moving through the trees.

"We have to go back," I gripped his shoulders as he broke into a run again, headed back to Haakon. But that way wasn't escape.

Ulf said nothing, only chose another direction. It was no use. Everywhere we turned, bushes crackled under hundreds of feet. The rank corpses filled the air with an overpowering stench.

I caught more and more glimpses of the Grey Men through the trees.

"Ulf," I pointed. He paused on a woody hill. Two groups of Grey Men converged and started to climb. I watched a way out disappear.

"They're hunting us," Ulf said grimly.

"They want me, right? I'll give myself up."

"Never." His arms tightened on me as he ran. But even I could tell we were being herded back the way we came.

"Wait," I said. "Put me down."

He hesitated and I hissed, "There is no time!"

Once on the ground, I tore off my gown. "Run with this," I said. "Spread my scent as far and wide as you can. If they must divide their forces, a way will clear."

He nodded. "Go back to Haakon." He pointed the way. "Hide."

When I arrived, breathless, back at camp, Haakon's brow wrinkled. "Lass?"

"Shhh," I crawled to his side. "We're surrounded. Ulf is distracting them."

"You must hide," he said. "I cannot reach Ulf—the Corpse King is blocking our bond. I fear you both lost your chance to get away."

"I wasn't about to leave you."

"You must. Go to the cliff, Laurel, find a place to hide. Ulf and I will fight as many as we can. Once their numbers are fewer—"

I shook my head "I won't survive without you."

"You must," Haakon growled. "Dammit, you must get out. Hide from the Grey Men. They hate water—"

"Is that all they fear?" I asked, with a glimmering of an idea.

"Well, Berserkers when there are enough of us. I will try to get word through to the Alphas that you are coming—"

"Haakon," I said as calmly as I could. The prickle up my spine told me the Grey Men were coming closer every moment. "I am not leaving you. You must tell me what to do. I am going to fight."

The warrior cursed.

I looked about. A few feet away, at the base of the ravine, the ground was wet. "The stream," I whispered.

"It's not enough, lass. The ground is damp but it won't be enough to keep the forces away."

"I don't care about the Grey Men," I scrambled towards Ulf's abandoned pack, praying it had what I needed. "I care about us."

A minute later, Haakon watched me blow onto a pile of pine needles. The blaze stared quickly enough. The ground across the ravine, under the pines was dry. And Ulf had left his flint and stone.

"There," I whispered, feeding my blaze with sticks

dipped in pitch. I ran along the dry feet of the trees, setting small fires where I could. With any luck, by the time the Grey Men came, a hearty blaze would screen Haakon and my escape.

I crept back to Haakon.

"Now what?"

"Now we wait." I winced as the fire crackled and sputtered, growing with each pitch dipped branch it devoured. The tree bark began to smoke.

"Ulf won't be able to come for you."

I winced, I knew the warrior feared fire. That's what had given me the idea.

"Go, lass. Climb the cliff as far as you can and hide."

I rose to my feet. "I won't go without you."

He sighed. "I can't walk, lass."

"I know." I bit my lip, but he was too big to drag. "If I carry the axe, can you crawl?"

ULF

The Grey Men marched on, hissing like snakes. I kept away from them, scenting instead a herd of deer that had waited too long to run. A burst of speed, and I surprised one, grabbing it and wrapping a piece of Laurel's red gown around it. The deer escaped, the fabric fluttering from its fragile leg red as a wound.

The last scrap of cloth was gone. The Grey Men were starting to swerve from their formation, chasing Laurel's scent tied to the wrong prey. Soon the deer would be slaughtered, and we'd lose our hold on this corner of the woods, but if I ran, we might have a chance to escape.

As I turned, a bitter scent choked me. A familiar crackling filled the air, magnified a thousand-fold. At my feet, beetles wriggled out of the wood and fled. Not away from the Grey Men. Towards them.

My skin prickled with old fear, and I knew what Laurel had done.

IN THE END, Haakon held the axe in his teeth as he crawled. His muscles strained and sweat poured down his bare back, but we moved closer to the cliff.

"There," I pointed. "There's a cave."

"Go," he gritted out between clenched teeth.

"I will, once you hide."

He sped up. I bit my lip and waited.

Behind us, the bonfire raged out of control. It had spread faster than I would've guessed, the flames eating up the dry tinder at the base of the pines. It hadn't crossed the wet patch of earth at the bottom of the ravine, yet.

I didn't dare breathe until Haakon crawled into the mouth of the small cave.

"I'll be all right, lass!" he called, clutching the axe. "It's damp enough here. Leave me. Climb the cliff—get to higher ground. Ulf will find you.

I ran out, and stopped dead. Grey Men emerged from the trees on the hill above the ravine, pale and stinking as maggots A hissing sound came from them, loud enough to contend with the fire. They held spears. If they came quickly, they could avoid the fire. The spears would reach Haakon and...

"Go, lass. What are you waiting for?"

"I'm the prize the Corpse King wants, right? The Grey Men will not hurt me."

"They will try to take you! Wait for Ulf—"

"I'm sorry," I muttered. "I cannot obey." Then I raised my voice and waved my hands, scrambling down the hill towards the fire. "Hey! Over here!"

The Grey Men poured from the tree line, headed in my direction. Some seemed to hesitate at the hot flames, but when one stumbled, another knocked it down and walked over it, taking its place.

"Come on," I shouted, and coughed. The smoke was growing thick. Bending over, I ran with streaming eyes until I found what I wanted. A long branch, its end dabbed with pitch. Grabbing it, I ran through the oven hot air, and thrust the branch into the blaze. It flared immediately.

The Grey Men could try to take me. They would burn.

Coughing on smoke, I took my torch and whirled towards my enemy.

"You want me? You can have me." Flaming torch high, I ran at the group of Grey Men. Several recoiled.

The Grey Man nearest to me lifted his spear so the end pointed skyward. I felt a rush of triumph. I was right; they would not dare kill me.

I thrust my torch at him, and confirmed my second hunch. Grey Men were corpses—old ones at that. The torch set the one before me alight.

Dry skin and bone crackled under the flame, crumbling to dust.

I screamed, and choked on the vile smoke.

The Grey Man fell, engulfed by flame. It rolled in the bush, spreading the fire to its comrades. Dead hands reached for me, and I set them all alight.

With hissing cries, the Grey Men fell under the fire.

Eyes and nose streaming, coughing, I ran back the way I came, but everywhere was fire.

"Laurel!" Ulf stood on the crest of the hill.

"Here," I shouted, throat raw, and shied as more bushes around me burst into flame. Any Grey Men left in this forest would burn.

I only hoped Haakon would not burn with them.

Ulf raced towards me, slowing as he avoided patches of flame. Sweat rolled down his body. His scarred face was a mask, but this time I could read his expression. Fear.

The sap in a pine tree exploded and I covered my head against the raining sparks.

"Laurel," Ulf called. "Come to me."

"Ulf, I can't! The flames."

"Come to me. I won't let you burn."

But when I ran towards him, the heat crackled in my face, hotter than the hottest oven. I thought I could bear it, but I could not.

With a roar, he ran through the fire to me. The creature who reached me was half man, half beast. The flames tore at his furred body.

He caught me and ran back up the hill. Past the trees, not falling as the fire consumed them from within. Past the flaming remains of the Grey Men. I kept an arm over my eyes to protect them from the smoke. The breath left my lungs, my skin blistered in the heat, but he held me close.

"Are you hurt? Are you burned?"

I clung to him.

I shook my head. It hurt to speak.

All around, the flames devoured the forest.

What had I done?

"Ulf—" I choked out, my throat raw and screaming for water, "we must get Haakon—"

"Too late."

And I realized what I done. I'd killed him. I'd killed my mate.

I dropped my arm, rolling in Ulf's arms to look back at the red waste. The world blurred. Smoke filled my lungs.

"Laurel? Laurel! Hang on—"

I let the darkness take me.

LAUREL

*S*omeone was calling out to me from the darkness. I had to
reach them--

I woke to cooling cloths suffusing my face.

"Ulf? Haakon—" I whimpered and thrashed, ripping at
the bandages like they were chains.

"Shhh, Laurel."

"Sister Juliet?" I recognized one of the nuns. She used to
be an orphan, but had taken vows.

"Just Juliet," she told me with a sad look. "The abbey is
no more."

I wanted to answer that her vows were still intact, but
she looked shaken, so I held my tongue.

"How are you feeling?" she asked. I lay in a lodge on a
soft bed, clad in a new, clean shift. My burns were bandaged
and my face felt chapped, but didn't throb too much.

"Where am I?" I croaked.

She lifted a horn of water to my lips and I drank.

"You're at the home of the Berserkers, along with all of
the captives."

"How many are here? Did they escape the Corpse King?

Where are my mates?"

Juliet hushed me, tipping the refilled cup up so I could drink.

"You've been asleep for a day and a night. A Berserker with a scarred face brought you in."

"That's Ulf," I said, eager for news. "Is he here? Was he badly hurt?"

"Perhaps another could answer questions better than I," she stepped back, looking so sad, I wanted to comfort her. But then I saw a familiar face poking around the tapestry lined enclosure where I lay.

"Hazel," I cried. The tanned, lovely face split into a grin. She stepped forward, clad in a fine gown, her hair twined with flowers and braided. She wore a torc around her neck and boots trimmed with fur. Her face glowed.

She jumped up onto the bed and hugged me tight.

"Laurel! You're alive—and well."

"So are you," I marveled at my friend. "I thought you were dead."

"We thought the same of you. The Corpse King attacked many as they left the abbey, but most escaped. My mate tells me often, not much can kill a Berserker."

I almost laughed at her imitation of a gruff warrior, remembering my own mates. Then I seized her arm. "Hazel, where are the others? Are they safe?"

"Many are. Sage and Willow have returned. Sister Juliet is watching over the young ones here. You were brought in unconscious from breathing smoke, but there are powerful healers here."

"And my mates? Haakon and Ulf? Is there word?"

Hazel's brow furrowed. My stomach turned.

"Please say something. Is Ulf at least here? May I speak to him?"

"I don't know, Laurel," Hazel grasped my hand. "Give me a moment. I will ask my mate." She closed her eyes and got a look of intent concentration I recognized from Ulf and Haakon, when I guessed they were speaking mind to mind. The seconds crawled by as I squeezed Hazel's hand.

Beyond the curtains surrounding my bed, young voices wafted up to the rafters, along with Sister Juliet's.

Hazel started, and blinked.

I couldn't stop myself from blurting, "You have a mate?"

"Yes," she said breathlessly, flushing a little. "He wasn't happy that I was asking him about another Berserker. I had to explain. He's, um, protective." The soft look in her face told me she loved it.

"Was he able to tell you..."

"Yes. Ulf carried you here, and left with a pack to find his warrior brother."

"And?"

"That's all my mate knows," Hazel whispered, "I'm so sorry."

I dashed at tears on my face. "It's all right. It was too much to hope."

"Keep hoping," she said. "And wait. Berserkers are strong. It's obvious you care for them very much."

"They are my mates," I said the words I'd fought for so long. It felt like something I'd known all along.

A shadow passed over my friend's face. "Hazel? What is it?"

"I didn't know you had bonded to anyone."

"I... I mean, I haven't. There's no link into their mind. But that can take a while to form, right?"

"It can," Hazel said slowly. "But that is not why I wondered whether or not you have a mate."

"I do have a mate. Ulf and... Haakon." If Haakon was still

alive.

There was a touch of pity in Hazel's face.

"Tell me," I begged.

"You're in the lodge for the unmated spaewives. Sister Juliet and the younger girls, none of them have been claimed. The Alphas decreed that a woman must go into heat before she can be claimed."

"But what does that have to do with me?"

"Ulf and Haakon built a lodge for their future mate. But Ulf brought you here. I'm sorry, Laurel. I don't think Ulf would've left you here, where any warrior might claim you, if he was truly your mate."

I RAN through the burning forest, dodging falling branches. The whole world was on fire. Soon it would come down on me.

"Ulf!" I screamed. "Haakon!"

"Laurel?" a faint whisper drew me through the gathering gloom. I started towards it, wading through the thick darkness like water.

"Haakon? I'm here. Tell me where you are," I begged. The world shrunk and I crawled through it like a tunnel. "I hear you breathing. I know you live. I will find you. Stay awake, my love. Stay awake!"

I woke with a start.

"How's she doing?" A voice beyond the curtain, muffled. Sister Juliet—or Juliet, as she insisted to be called— answered in a voice too low for me to hear.

I did not know how much time had past since Hazel left my side. It did not matter. My life, my time no longer mattered.

Haakon was missing, and thought to be dead. Ulf had

left me to be claimed by another.

I rolled to my side, empty of tears. I wished to god I hadn't set that fire. Ulf hated fire. How much more did he hate me for killing his warrior brother with one?

"Laurel?" Hazel pulled back the curtain. "There are two here who want to see you."

The two turned out to be Sage and Willow, my old friends. Fine gowns, fur boots, flushed faces: the very image of Berserker brides. I embraced them but didn't feign happiness.

"Oh, Laurel," Sage stroked my hair. With her pink cheeks and flaxen hair, she looked much healthier than when I last saw her, as if she'd been eating well for weeks, not just days.

"You're looking so well," I murmured, unwilling to face anymore pity.

"My mates," she said, blushing. "They like to...care for me."

Willow and Sage told me their stories while I dressed. The old Laurel wouldn't believe their tales. So much had changed for all of us. We had changed. We weren't the same girls in the abbey, anymore.

Sage had finished and sat brushing my hair when Juliet interrupted, looking harried. "Laurel, can you help me?"

"Of course." I hastened to follow.

"Our captors brought us food. But—" She waved a hand at the large carcass lying next to the hearth.

"I see," I said. "Hazel, can your mate better prepare this for us?"

"Yes, but not here. None of the Berserkers are allowed to come in here, on pain of death. The Alphas decree," Hazel explained.

"They could've at least skinned it." Willow prodded the

dead game with her foot.

"This isn't the first time we were delivered raw meat. In fact, meat is all we have had to eat. Perhaps your... mate," Juliet's nose flared in distaste at the word, "will find us more suitable food. We are not used to such a rich diet."

Hazel drew herself up. "I'm sure our saviors," she emphasized the word, "will be happy to provide whatever we need."

"No need to fight," Sage murmured. "We're on the same side."

Juliet nodded stiffly. She wore a sturdy gown much like ours, but had covered her hair with a veil as the abbey nuns did. Her eyes looked a little red. "In the meantime, what shall we eat?"

"I can make a porridge," I told them, "If you will give me a pot and the grains."

"Oh, Laurel makes the best porridge," Clover, one of the young ones, spoke up. "She even puts plums in it."

"I don't know if we can get plums," I said.

"The Berserkers can get anything," Hazel said. "Though it is harder right now, with the Alphas restricting travel because of the Corpse King."

"Who?" one of the other young girls asked.

"A king, dearest," Juliet stepped in. "He's at war with these... warriors."

"We'll explain more later," Hazel said, raising a brow at Juliet. "They need to know at some point."

Juliet gave a stiff nod. "Come," she told her charges. "Let us see if the guards will let us go to the meadow to pick daisies again."

"What is wrong with Juliet?" I asked as soon as the place was clear.

"I don't know," Sage frowned.

Hazel shrugged. "She is unhappy that she is here."

"Where are the other nuns?"

"They were given a choice to come or run. Juliet was the only one who chose to stay—to watch over the younger girls and do what she could to protect them. The rest ran to save their own skin."

"I'm glad they aren't here," Willow announced. "They were cruel to us."

I shivered, remembering some of the punishments.

"They probably didn't survive," Sage said softly. "The Corpse King turned all the men of the village into Grey Men, and attacked the abbey. And then there was a great earthquake. The place was destroyed." She raised her eyes to the three of us gaping at her. "Or so my mates tell me."

"I shall ask Juliet if she is well. The Alphas won't allow her to be mistreated," Willow said.

"It's too dangerous for us out there, anyway," Hazel huffed. "The Corpse King is desperate to rise to power. At least here, we are safe. No one will care for us like the Berserkers."

I pressed my lips together. Hazel had almost been sacrificed to the Corpse King, and barely escaped when her mate rescued her. She had a different opinion of the Berserkers than the spaewives who'd been carried off in the middle of the night. Of course, Willow and Sage were also happily mated. I decided I'd talk to Juliet myself. If anything, it'd take my mind off Haakon and Ulf.

"So, where is this porridge?" I asked, looping my arms through Sage and Willow's.

"We'll show you," Hazel brightened. "There's a place here you might like to see. A sort of gift to you from the Berserkers."

Hazel led us from the lodge, ignoring the guard left by

the door until he lowered his staff in front of her.

"You cannot leave."

"I can. My mate is waiting for me."

"So are ours," Willow said, though she didn't look the Berserker in the eye. Sage played with the torc around her neck, eyes downcast.

"She is unmated," the guard pointed at me. His words hit me like a blow. I stared back at him, until Willow grabbed my hand, whispering, "Eyes down."

"We will escort her, and our mates will escort us. No one will get close to her. Unless you mean to…" Hazel pulled me forward, so my breasts almost touched the staff the warrior held. The guard yanked the staff up, flushing. I met his eyes boldly, and he jerked his head away, and didn't stop us when we walked out.

"Come on," Hazel tugged me along. I went reluctantly. For a moment I'd been distracted from my miserable thoughts of Ulf and Haakon. The guard had been a bit silly, but cute.

"No wonder there have been so many petitions to court you," Willow muttered.

"What?" I drew my gaze away from the guard.

Sage shrugged. "The Berserkers can tell you've come into your heat."

Three more guards hovered on the edge of the field where Juliet and the young ones sat making daisy chains. On this fine, warm day, they were heavily armed, and alert, as if expecting attack.

"The guards aren't allowed to get too close," Hazel told me. "And there are at least four of them present, perhaps more hidden in the woods. Morning, noon, and night. The Corpse King might never venture here, but the Alphas say we can't be too careful."

The home of the unmated spaewives was on a rocky ridge in an isolated part of the mountain. To reach the main paths, we had to climb around huge boulders, and make our way over a bridge stretched across a ravine.

"It's like they're protecting some precious treasure," I muttered as we crossed the bridge.

Sage glanced back at me, her skirts lifted in her dainty hands. "They are."

Two more guards waited at the bottom of the bridge, spears in hand.

Hazel waved to someone I couldn't see—a shadow in the woods. "My mate," she explained. "He's escorting us today, but Willow and Sage's mates don't want him too close to them."

I nodded, trying to pretend I was glad I didn't have men so jealous of my attention. My three friends led me down a winding path, pointing out the way to the stream and their own lodges along the way. The day was fresh and fine. Between my friends and the flowers dancing in the breeze, I almost forgot the war being raged beyond the sunny mountain. The Corpse King had routed several bands of Berserkers and the spaewives they escorted. The Alphas had patrols combing the countryside for the missing men. I still had no word whether Haakon was alive, and Ulf... well, there was a reason the guards thought I was unmated.

"Here it is!" Hazel tore up the slope ahead of us. The lodge rose from a flower-filled meadow, angled away from the forest to face a sweeping vista. Picking up my skirts, I climbed past newly hewn stumps, and followed a trail of wood chips to a large room built off the side of the lodge. The bright logs and the scent of new wood told me the place had just been built.

"Do you like it?"

I wandered through the wide space. A great stone hearth dominated the wall the room shared with the rest of the lodge. A door opened to the dark depths beyond, but Hazel didn't venture back there, so I didn't mention it. The room held enough to interest me. Sturdy counters lined the walls, and two large trestle tables sat in the middle of the room. Two doors and a long row of open air windows lent plenty of light.

"Well?" Hazel asked.

"It's very nice," I murmured, wondering why she'd brought me here.

Sage and Willow entered, baskets in hand. Grinning, they hung bundles of herbs from the hooks on the lower rafters. Hazel reached under a few counters and pulled out bowls and platters.

Realization dawned. "It's a kitchen."

"Yes," Sage dusted herb leaves off her hands, and laid a basket full of apples on the trestle table.

"The Berserkers built it for you. The lodge was here, but they added this."

I ran my hand over the beautiful stone mantel. The fire place was large enough to spit a boar—or two. "Why?"

Hazel shrugged. "We've spoken of the food you made. The Alphas must've thought it a good idea to give you a place to work now that there are more mouths to feed."

I sat down on the hearth, overcome. The building was beyond anything I'd ever dreamed of. I could be happy here. Spend my days in the kitchens, cooking whatever I liked. Evenings with my friends, feeding them good food. But my nights would be alone.

A whistle made me jump.

"Delivery for the cook," a deep voice said. Willow and Sage backed away from the door as a Berserker came in, muscles straining as he raised a trussed piece of game. "Where do you want it?"

"Uh, just there," I pointed. He smiled and laid his bundle down on a table. It was a boar, no doubt a good, fresh kill.

"Thank you," I told him. He grinned and dipped his head, loping off.

My friends all had smiles. I noted they averted their eyes from the warrior.

"Be careful who you look at, Laurel," Hazel warned when the warrior was out of earshot.

"Why?"

"The only men we may look upon are our mates," Sage explained.

I made an annoyed sound.

"It's not so bad, when you get used to it," Willow said with a rueful smile. "Looking at the warriors encourages them."

"Unless you want to encourage them?" Hazel asked.

"No," I said quickly.

"Then be careful," Sage said. "Our mates don't like us looking at other men. Perhaps one day, when most of the warriors are mated and they live as civilized men, instead of beasts. But for now, we follow the rules or submit to punishment."

"Of course, the Berserkers seem to enjoy punishing their mates," Willow added, and we all blushed.

To hide my feelings, I fussed with the warrior's offering. Boar—Haakon's favorite meat. My throat closed.

"Are you all right?" Hazel asked.

I jerked my head up and down.

"I'll need some herbs to properly dress this. Do you think your mate will escort us into the woods to forage?"

"Of course," Hazel said after a pause. "I have started a garden—I would like to show you. Nothing's been planted yet, but Knut has turned the soil to make it ready. He complains of turning his best spear into a hoe." She laughed.

"I should like to have a garden too," Willow said. "The men do well enough on mostly raw meat, but I long for some new dishes."

"Yes, you must tell us what herbs are good for seasoning, Laurel. That is what we will grow first," Sage said.

"Leave by that way," Hazel pointed to a small door to the left of the hearth. "It leads straight to the woods, and a stream."

Taking up a bucket, Sage started to exit, and almost tripped over a bundle of dead rabbits left on the stoop.

"For you, Laurel. More offerings to the queen of the kitchens," Hazel smiled.

"Word spreads fast," Willow murmured to Sage.

Something in her tone made me turn. "What do you mean?"

"These rabbits, this meat. It's a gift for you."

"I don't understand. Why do they give those to me?"

"They hope to tempt you to become their mate."

I inhaled a sharp breath.

Willow and Sage filed out, taking care stepped over the rabbits.

Hazel gave me a sympathetic look. "Hang them high. I'll ask my mate to skin it for you."

I didn't want to touch these offerings from other men. But meat was meat. With a sigh, I took up my gift, and did as Hazel suggested.

∼

TWO DAYS LATER, I'd spent almost every waking minute in the kitchen. The lodge itself remained silent and empty; I peeked in there, but didn't want to disturb whomever lived there. Though I never saw anyone, I felt grateful they shared their hearth with me. The kitchen was fast becoming my home.

A giant vat of porridge simmered slowly, ready for a Berserker to carry it to the lodge of unmated spaewives. I served it sweetened with plums and honey. Sage joined me for hours on end, helping me peel and chop and grind herbs. Willow and Hazel also visited, bearing baskets of mushrooms and hard apples they found in the woods. And, often, Berserker warriors came by, leaving gifts of meat for me.

Around sunset, a great whoop went up on the mountain, loud enough to reach my ears. I left the fire and stepped into the cool evening air.

"What is it?" I asked Hazel, who'd been hoeing a patch of earth beyond the door for a kitchen garden.

"A band of warriors have returned," she said, wiping sweat from her face. A second later she broke into a smile.

"Laurel!" Willow shouted from the woods, racing up to me. "Did you hear? Haakon has been found!"

I staggered, and Sage came from table to put her arm around me.

"My mates tells me the warriors found him deep in a cave—he dragged himself there to escape the fire. He was badly injured, but Sabine is working on healing him now. Soon he will be well enough to move."

"That is great news." I embraced my friends, feeling cold in my heart.

"Do you feel them, at all?" Sage asked. "Through the bond?"

Three pairs of shining eyes pinned me. I could only shake my head. "Not yet."

"You will," Hazel said, but before she could offer more encouragement, a giant Berserker stepped from the trees, and she ran to kiss her mate.

Murmuring assurances, I went back to the hearth.

There was to be a celebration. My friends stayed with me as long as they could, but one by one they left as their mates came for them. They promised to return to help carry the food down to the great bonfire. All available Berserkers were hunting for deer, pig, and pheasant to roast over the open flame, but the spaewives were eager to taste my baking.

The sun glimmered low in the sky when I stood in the door and stretched. I'd worked all day, and was almost done. In the great hearth, the boar cooked with an apple in its mouth. I'd lined the counters with cooling loaves of bread, and tray after tray of honey cakes.

Someone had left a parcel on my doorstep. Hoping it was not more meat, I stooped and brought it inside, marveling at its light weight. I cut the twine, and caught my breath. Beautiful folds of fabric spilled from the package. The cloth was red as ripe currants.

I thought the color would suit your pale skin and dark hair.

Goosebumps running up and down my arms, I ducked into the empty lodge. Surely the owner wouldn't mind me changing in there. I washed in a little water, and braided my long hair. The gown fit like a dream. The smooth folds swirled around my legs. My reflection in the washing basin made me catch my breath.

I returned to tidy the kitchen, but the prickling on my arms didn't go away.

"Hello? Is someone there?" I turned, but saw no one.

Someone had come in, though. They'd left a head of cabbage on my chopping table. I picked it up, examining it as if it could tell me who'd brought it.

"Like my gift?"

A shock went through me at the familiar voice. I whirled around.

Haakon stood grinning at me. He looked a bit thinner than the man who'd carried me from the abbey, but no illness had touched his charm or his dimple.

I couldn't speak. I threw myself at Haakon. His arms slid around me instantly.

"Careful lass," he said. "I'm still not up to full strength."

But when I tried to back away, he held me close. I pressed my face into his chest.

"I thought you were dead. I left you—"

"Just a bit of fire."

Sobs shook me. Haakon was here. He was alive. He bent over me, soothing me as I buried my face in the crook of his neck. His hands roamed up and down my back, bringing my body to life. I'd be happy if I never had to leave the circle of his arms again.

I raised my head long enough to ask, "How—?"

"Ulf came back for me. I passed out, woke to him calling to me." He stroked my hair. "I saw you. In a dream."

"I dreamt of you too. You were hurt in a dark place. I called you back."

He smiled again, gently, and I traced his dimple. "We shared the dream. You and I, and Ulf too. He knew where to look for me. The fire left no trace of my trail, but I'd crawled deeper into the cave and he found me there. He couldn't reach me via the bond, but the dream gave him hope. He wouldn't have found me if it weren't for you."

I gazed into his eyes for a moment before I realized what

he was saying to me. "We shared a dream. Does that mean—?"

"Yes, Laurel. The bond has formed."

I drew back, trembling. It was too much to hope.

"Laurel? What is wrong?"

"He left me," I whispered, my gut twisting. "They told me he renounced his claim. I live with the unmated women. Warriors bring me gifts now, to gain my favor..."

Haakon growled deep in his chest. I jerked back, but he kept hold of me, forcing me to face him. "Do you want another mate?"

"I—"

Haakon snarled, his eyes bright, his canines elongated. "Do you? Tell me."

"No. There is no one else."

"Who would you choose over us?"

"No one," I cried. "I choose you."

His grip relaxed. As tight as it'd gotten, I knew he'd never hurt me.

"I thought you didn't want me."

"Oh, love," he pulled me into his arms. "I'm sorry. This is Ulf's doing. He does not think he is fit to be your mate. He thinks you will not forgive him for leaving me. If I had died, he wanted you to be free to choose another."

"What?" It was my turn to growl. "Ulf saved me from the fire. I wouldn't be alive without him. Without both of you. I thought," I choked on the painful knot inside me. "I thought he was angry with me. For setting the fire—"

"No, lass, 'twas a brave thing you did. The fire killed all the Grey Men. It saved me. And now we have more weapons to fight the Corpse king's servants. Not that you'll be fighting. You're a Berserker bride now."

"Where is Ulf?" I asked, my body still humming with anger, with joy, with pain. "Bring me to him."

"I will," Haakon said. "But first tell me if you like my gift."

"The gown? It's lovely."

"Not the gown," he scoffed. "I brought you the cabbage."

"Then who..."

"See, Ulf?" Haakon called. "I told you she'd prefer your gift to mine. Come out, so she can thank you properly."

I held my breath as Ulf stepped inside. His face was rough with stubble, and his eyes looked tired, but they lit when they landed on me. My heart squeezed. He was so beautiful to me, even his scar.

"Go to him," Haakon murmured, and I was moving before he finished speaking, racing to Ulf. I couldn't help it. I had to touch him.

Ulf jerked to a stop as I approached. I lay my hands on his chest, ran them over his shoulder and back.

"Are you hurt?" I murmured when he stayed stiff and still.

"No. Not anymore."

I cupped his face, meeting his eyes.

"Thank you."

"For saving you? Or for saving your mate?"

"For coming for me. Now...and before. In the abbey kitchens."

His arms closed around me slowly. "I will always come for you, if you wish it."

"And I will always wish it," I whispered. He didn't soften to my touch but he would. "So, now. We are mated? Will you bring me to your lodge?"

Ulf blinked. "What do you mean?"

"The home you built for your mate. Will you bring me

there? And mark me, and give me a torc around my neck? So that others might know that I am claimed?"

"Oh we will," Haakon growled, coming up behind me. He pressed into my back, and I felt how my words had affected him. "We will do all those things, and more."

"As for our lodge, lass..." Ulf spread his hands. "You are here. This is ours. As soon as I was able to link to the pack, I told them to build the kitchens for you."

"Did no one tell you?"

"No," I thumped his arms. "Other Berserkers have been bringing me meat! My friends told me you'd renounced your claim."

"I thought, if Haakon was lost, you might wish to choose another. I would've let you," Ulf said.

"I don't want another," I didn't know whether to cry or scream. "I want you."

"You are beautiful." His fingers sifted through my hair. In his eyes, I saw such longing.

"You told me you would bind me to you forever," I whispered.

"I will," he promised.

"You already have."

I surged onto my tiptoes, wrapping my arms around his neck. As soon as I tilted up my face, his lips crashed down on mine. His arousal dug into my belly until he lifted me, pulling my legs around his strong trunk.

We kissed until Haakon cleared his throat. Untwining my legs, I let Ulf guide me to the ground.

"So that is settled." I straightened my gown.

"Not quite," Haakon said. "As you say, other Berserkers have been trying to lay claim to you. We've been hearing all sorts of talk. You've been flirting with all manner of warriors, and looking them in the eye."

"Oh that stupid rule," I rolled my eyes.

"The rule that helps us keep our beast in check?" Ulf raised a brow.

"They say you've shown interest in several warriors, and cooked their meat."

"Of course I cooked the meat they brought. It's perfectly good meat."

"So you don't deny you encouraged others to court you?"

I looked from one stern face to another and threw up my hands. "Well, after you abandoned me, what did you expect? I would lie about moping until you returned? It's not my fault that every strong unmated warrior wants me —oof!"

The air left my stomach as Ulf and Haakon lifted me, setting me on the counter as if I was a piece of meat. I scrambled back on the wooden surface, putting the whole table between me and the bright eyed warriors.

"So you've decided to cross us? Defy your mates once again?" Haakon's grin flashed his long canines. Ulf stalked around the counter toward me.

"Perhaps," I slipped to the ground and backed away, my hands searching for something I could use as a weapon. "You said you like spirited women."

"No," Haakon cocked his head to the side. "We said we liked you. But you've been a very naughty mate. Running from us, arguing with us, grabbing up torches and going into battle when we specifically told you to flee—"

"That saved your life!"

"You're a Berserker bride now. And Berserkers bring their mates to heel."

"You can try," I growled. My hands closed on a missile and I threw it without thinking. Haakon narrowly avoided being hit in the head with a cabbage.

"There she is," Ulf murmured. "The fighter in the kitchens."

Haakon straightened and I grabbed up an apple. A pause, while the warriors debated what to do, and I held my breath.

"All right, lass," Haakon announced. "We've decided that Ulf will discipline you, and I will watch. You mustn't worry that I'm depriving myself. After he finishes punishing you, it's my turn to take you to task, and Ulf will watch.

"If you think I will submit to that willingly, you are much mistaken."

"Oh little love," his eyes glittered. "I very much hope you won't."

A minute later, the kitchen was a riot of thrown apples and fallen platters, the floor liberally dusted with flour.

I lay naked, trussed like a piece of game with my hands tied behind my back.

"Here's something to keep your mouth occupied," Haakon said, and stuck an apple in my mouth—one of the tiny ones, too small to be poached. I was saving it for decoration. Too bad I'd never thought I'd be the centerpiece. My nipples dug into the hard table at the thought of being brought out and displayed thus for an entire meal.

"You'll learn to mind us, Laurel," Haakon said as Ulf checked his knots. "Until then, we'll tie you up so you can't leave.

"And for your punishment?" Ulf said. "I think we have found the perfect implement." He waved a wooden spoon in front of my face.

The two warriors took their time securing me, laying me just as they wished on the table, cupping my curves and speaking of me as if I was a new fancy they'd bought at market. Waves of arousal rippled through me. My ears filled with the sound of my heavy breathing, and the kitchen was filled with my musky scent.

"Please," I said finally. "Get it over with."

"I love it when she begs for punishment," Ulf remarked.

"I love it when she begs for anything at all."

The first bite of the spoon made my eyes bug out. The apple popped from my mouth as I shouted.

"It hurts!"

"Naughty lass," Ulf replaced the apple with a few loops of rope tied to the harness crisscrossing my body. "Most spaewives take their punishment like good submissives, then kneel down to thank their mates."

Clenching my jaw, I dug my teeth into the rope.

"I doubt this one will kneel. But she is definitely a spaewife. Look at how she responds to a little pain." Haakon ran his fingers through my wet cunny lips, and showed the sticky digits to me before licking them clean. "Give her a little more, Ulf, and see how she creams."

The spoon popped my bottom in quick succession. I sucked in a breath, determined not to make a fuss. My mates enjoyed it too much.

"Try this," Haakon picked up a long handled bread paddle. As soon as it cracked against my bottom I shouted loud enough to bring everyone on the mountain running.

"Such sweetness," Haakon said, dipping his fingers into my cunny. I moaned.

"Try it on this," Ulf said.

"A carrot? What do you think I am, a rabbit?"

"Suit yourself," Ulf said, and slid the cold, hard object inside me. The gag muffled my outraged shouts as he twisted it around, stimulating every part of my opening.

"See," he said, after fucking me with the carrot and withdrawing it. "Tastes sweet."

"Let me try." Haakon's mischievous tone made me stiffen. He was up to something, but I could only lie here and take it.

A second later oil poured over the cleft of my bottom. All my wriggling couldn't encourage the knots holding me to budge. A finger delved between my slippery cheeks, testing and rimming my back hole before another unyielding object—I could only assume the carrot—took its place. The tip slid in, my tight rosebud stretching with unnatural sensation as the carrot tapered wider. It didn't hurt. I felt strange, and full. Arousal fluttered in my belly even as I kicked and shrieked and protested.

"Careful, honey," Ulf curled his arm around me. "I don't want these ropes to mark you."

"Honey. Now that's a good idea. Is there any about?" Leaving the carrot in my asshole, Haakon went on the hunt.

"Say you'll yield," Ulf whispered, stroking my hair, "And your punishment will be over."

"Nuh-uh," I tossed my head, snarling at him. I was done being a good girl.

"Suit yourself," he moved and Haakon took his place.

"Do you like having your bottom stuffed?"

I bared my teeth at him. He just laughed. "You better get used to it. We're having a plug made. You'll wear it whenever we see fit, all day while you make your fancy cakes. We'll have you bend over and show it to us whenever we please." He leaned in close. "And when we take it out, we'll replace it with our cocks."

A whimper escaped. He patted my bottom, twisting the carrot in further. "Soon you'll beg us to fill you in this way. You'll see."

Already my arousal crashed over me, fierce waves of desire. But when Ulf and Haakon lifted me by the rope harness and flipped me over, baring my body to them, I saw the hunger in their eyes. And when Haakon lifted the honey comb and let the sweet stuff drizzle on my bound breasts, need swelled within me, stealing my thought, taking my breath away. Two hot mouths closed over my breasts, licking and sucking my nipples to peaks. I writhed in the ropes, my desire ballooning because I couldn't move to express it. Endless whimpers escaped me. If I could speak I would've been saying, "Please."

"So sweet." Haakon turned me so he stood between my legs. His mouth fastened onto my leaking cunny, swirling around my pleasure spot until lights exploded behind my eyes. I bit down on the rope as my climax roared through me.

The next instant I sprawled out on the table as Ulf sliced through the ropes and let them fall away.

"Please," I begged. "Take me."

"Little love," Haakon climbed onto the table to kneel between my legs. "We thought you'd never ask." Pausing only to pull out the carrot, he caught my legs behind my knees to lift them, and impaled me. My head fell back as my wet heat engulfed him.

"Me as well." Ulf stood at the table end, his cock at the perfect height for my mouth. I sucked him inside. He plucked at my nipples, sending heat spiraling through me. Haakon moved between my legs, his thrusts rocking me onto Ulf's cock.

Then I was yanked upright, pulled free as the trestle table crashed to the ground. Ulf held me safe, and Haakon had sprung away just in time. The large slab of wood hit its twin, knocking it over too.

When the dust settled, Haakon's laugh rang around the room.

"You broke my tables," I gasped. The kitchen was a mess —I'd thrown every pot and hard apple I could grab, and my mates had shielded themselves with trays. And now the great, sturdy tables lay askew, knocked over by my mate's hard thrusting.

Good thing I'd put the honey cakes on the counter.

"Are you hurt?"

I shook my head.

"We'll clean the mess and put this place to rights," Haakon assured me.

"Later," Ulf growled, catching my arm. "We aren't done." He drew me to the hearth. "Put your hands on the stone."

I folded in half, taking the position that bared my vulnerable backside to them. I waited a few breaths, and looked back. Ulf and Haakon hadn't moved, couldn't tear their eyes off me. Smiling, I waved my arse in the air until Ulf snapped out of trance.

"Oil," he said, and when I pointed, told me to turn back around.

"Breathe," Haakon instructed, coming to lay a soothing hand on my back.

Oil spilled liberally over my bottom and cleft. I tried not to squirm as Ulf slicked his fingers and twisted one, then two into my bottom hole, stretching me.

"Brace yourself and open to me," Ulf ordered.

"Breathe," Haakon repeated.

I splayed my hands on the grey stone, and tried to do what my stern mate wished. He scooted my legs further apart, and grasped my hips to pull them higher. His rod brushed my back hole. I tensed.

"Not like that. Open to me."

Haakon sat beside me, stroking himself. His cock waved close to my face as Ulf's breached my asshole, stretching the tight ring of muscle. With the oil, it slid forward easily, burning a little. Ulf alternately pushed and withdrew, making his way. My cunny pulsed as he filled the most intimate part of me.

"How is it?" Haakon asked him.

A gasp from Ulf.

"That good?" Haakon winked and gave me his dimple.

Ulf pulled out and stroked my back, giving me a rest. "So sweet, to give yourself fully to us."

I reached back and touched the iron muscle in his leg. He was so strong, to be so gentle. Curving my back, I arched my head back. "Take me."

Curses fell from his lips as he pushed in fully. My cunny gushed when Ulf's cock was seated in the depths of my bowels. His hand came round to stroke me and my legs shook.

"Oh no." I denied the dark sensation. I could not climax from this.

"Yes, Laurel. Submit to us. Submit to your mates."

His fingers pushed me higher until my knees gave out and he fully supported me. Haakon watched with bright eyes, his laughter gone and replaced by pure hunger.

A log popped and sent spark showering close to my face and I cried out. Instantly, I was up in Ulf's arms, one strong forearm across my belly. The other hand slid to cup my throat.

"Don't worry. I've got you. I've always got you."

Haakon moved before me, blocking my view of the fire. His hands cupped my breasts, plucked my nipples before dipping between my legs to rub my sweet spot again. Ulf held me captive, and between Haakon's skilled fingers and Ulf's powerful hand cradling my pulse, I climbed the heights of pleasure again.

Just before I tipped over, Haakon took his hands away.

Ulf tightened his hold. "Now, brother."

Haakon cocked a leg on the hearth and guided himself into my sopping wet heat. He slid in slowly, filling me inch by scant inch, holding my eyes the whole time.

"Wait for it," Ulf ordered, and I fought back my orgasm until both men were joined to me, touching the deepest parts of me, overwhelming me with sensation.

On the edge of orgasm, my body held its breath. Haakon began to thrust.

Now, Ulf's voice reverberated through my mind, filling the last part of me. Haakon's cry joined his. I broke on their cocks, shuddering with pleasure, only their strong arms, the press of their skin against mine kept me from shattering.

Teeth pierced my neck. Haakon reared his head back, canines flashing, and snapped down onto my shoulder. The twin bites of pain made me explode with pleasure. The men never stopped thrusting.

Mine, their voices echoed in my head. *Ours. Now and forever.*

I added my own hoarse cry, undulating between them, tossed to and fro in a storm of sensation. My body cracked and splintered, all that I was pouring out. But it didn't disappear. I was not destroyed. Somehow, I was more.

Ulf and Haakon slammed into me, touching my very core. I swam in their arms, dizzy, happy, spent, as they cursed through their climax. The sore points on my shoulders tingled. Somehow I knew the bites would heal quickly, but I'd always bear a scar. A mark. Proof I was owned.

Laurel. Haakon's lips found mine. I clutched at him with my left arm, sliding a hand back to Ulf. My right hand brushed the harsh ridge of his scar, and he jerked back, sliding from my body and setting me on the floor. Ulf still was not comfortable around me. No matter. I was Laurel, mate of the Berserkers. Fully myself, unwilling to hide. I'd shine my love on him until there was nothing ugly left, only Ulf.

Are you ready for us to take you to bed? Haakon's voice filled my mind.

My head snapped around.

"What is it, lass?"

"I heard you," I breathed. "Inside my head."

Yes, little love. 'Tis the bond. Come, lass. It's time we had you in our home.

"Wait." I tugged from his hold. "The boar, the honey cakes. I was to bring this food to the feast."

"We sent word we were claiming you," Ulf said. "Tonight, the pack can cook their own feast."

"I'll eat the boar," Haakon offered. "And you like honey cakes."

My mouth fell open. "There are hundreds of them."

"Yes, well," Haakon came up behind me, squeezing my breasts. "You will need all this food to have the stamina to satisfy your mates."

Much later, when they'd showed me the rest of the lodge, particularly the bed, I lay swirling my fingers over Haakon's chest. He smiled even in sleep, his dimple winking at me.

"How was he when you found him?" I asked Ulf.

"Unconscious. At first I was afraid he'd done more damage to his back. But the healing had gone well. He just needed food and water. He'll heal faster now, with the bond between us complete."

I pondered this. There was much I did not understand about the mating bond. Tomorrow, I would ask my friends.

Beside me, Ulf let out a long sigh. I bit my lip.

"What is it, Laurel?" he said without opening his eyes.

I jumped at his voice.

After all this time, do you still fear me? As our minds connected, I felt his wistful longing.

"Of course not." But a part of me still cringed.

"Tell me, little one."

"Are you angry with me... for the fire?"

"No." He rolled towards me, settling his large body over mine. His muscled arms held him aloft. His hands rested on either side of my face, his thumbs brushing my jaw. In a cocoon of his heat and his attention, I couldn't hide. My heart cracked a little, pain pouring into the bond between us.

"You left me," I whispered. Silently I shared every cringe, every cold moment I felt on the mountain when the Berserkers and my friends made it clear I'd been abandoned by my mates.

He didn't answer, just stroked my hair back from my cheeks. "So lovely," he murmured. "A woman like you can have any man she wanted."

"Not any man. The one I wanted renounced his claim on me."

His eyes closed. "I thought only to set you free."

Anger flashed through me. "You didn't have the right—"

"I'm ugly." He said it without wincing, but I felt it deep in his heart just the same. His body hovered so close, but it took all my courage to touch him.

"To me you are the most handsome of men," I whispered, my fingertips light on his chest.

His gaze slid away. But for once, he forgot to turn the unmarred side of his face to me. I studied the rough web of skin that made up his cheek, sunken below his eye. And I knew what to say.

"I would not love you as much without your scars." I opened myself to him via the bond, so he would know every word was true.

"You pity—"

I put a finger to his lips. "You saved me. You and Haakon both... but you walked through fire for me, knowing what it's like to be burned."

He met my gaze. Scarred and handsome, fierce and gentle. My mate.

"None of the Berserkers who courted me could even compare."

Ulf clutched me, a growl deep in his chest.

"But I couldn't even think of them, not when I had the bravest man on the Earth lay claim to me. Even if you'd returned without Haakon, I wouldn't have been able to rest until I'd claimed you."

Mate. He gripped the back of my neck, holding me still for his lips. It wasn't a kiss, it was a plunder. He took and took, and I tipped my head back and gave, for I had endless love to give.

He rolled off me, and I tucked into his side, face to face.

No more hiding. I touched his scarred cheek.

Never again. He took my promise as I took his.

I snuggled into him as Haakon began to snore. *I hope our children will be like you.*

Ulf stiffened. "Children," he whispered.

"Yes." I clung to him, not daring to ask whether he wanted a child.

"They will not be burned," he said in wonder. "They will have my face, but none of my scars."

I bit my lip, blinking back tears at his awe. I gripped his shoulder fiercely. "I don't care how they look, as long as they have your courage. I want their heart as big as their father's."

"And their mother's." He twined his hand with mine.

I pressed into him. "You will teach them to be brave, Ulf."

"We both will." He kissed my hair, and with that final promise, we joined Haakon in sleep.

Nine months later, my son Ulfarr, a spitting image of his father, was born.

***

The Berserker Saga

Sold to the Berserkers - – Brenna, Samuel & Daegan
Mated to the Berserkers - – Brenna, Samuel & Daegan
Bred by the Berserkers (FREE novella only available at www.leesavino.com) - – Brenna, Samuel & Daegan
Taken by the Berserkers – Sabine, Ragnvald & Maddox
Given to the Berserkers – Muriel and her mates
Claimed by the Berserkers – Fleur and her mates

Berserker Brides

Rescued by the Berserker – Hazel & Knut
Captured by the Berserkers – Willow, Leif & Brokk
Kidnapped by the Berserkers – Sage, Thorbjorn & Rolf
Bonded to the Berserkers – Laurel, Haakon & Ulf
Berserker Babies – the sisters Brenna, Sabine, Muriel, Fleur and their mates
Night of the Berserkers – the witch Yseult's story
Owned by the Berserkers – Fern, Dagg & Svein
Tamed by the Berserkers — Sorrel, Thorsteinn & Vik
Mastered by the Berserkers — Juliet, Jarl & Fenrir

FREE BOOK

Get a secret Berserker book, Bred by the Berserkers (only to the awesomesauce fans on Lee's email list)
Go here to get started... https://geni.us/BredBerserker

ALSO BY LEE SAVINO

Ménage Sci Fi Romance

Draekons (Dragons in Exile) with Lili Zander (ménage alien dragons)

Crashed spaceship. Prison planet. Two big, hulking, bronzed aliens who turn into dragons. The best part? The dragons insist I'm their mate.

Paranormal romance

Bad Boy Alphas with Renee Rose (bad boy werewolves)

Never ever date a werewolf.

Sci fi romance

Draekon Rebel Force with Lili Zander

Start with Draekon Warrior

Tsenturion Warriors with Golden Angel

Start with Alien Captive

Contemporary Romance

Royal Bad Boy

I'm not falling in love with my arrogant, annoying, sex god boss. Nope. No way.

Royally Fake Fiancé

The Duke of New Arcadia has an image problem only a fiancé can fix.

And I'm the lucky lady he's chosen to play Cinderella.

Beauty & The Lumberjacks

After this logging season, I'm giving up sex. For...reasons.

Her Marine Daddy

My hot Marine hero wants me to call him daddy...

Her Dueling Daddies

Two daddies are better than one.

Innocence: dark mafia romance with Stasia Black

I'm the king of the criminal underworld. I always get what I want. And she is my obsession.

Beauty's Beast: a dark romance with Stasia Black

Years ago, Daphne's father stole from me. Now it's time for her to pay her family's debt...with her body.

ABOUT THE AUTHOR

Lee Savino is a USA today bestselling author. She's also a mom and a choco-holic. She's written a bunch of books—all of them are "smexy" romance. Smexy, as in "smart and sexy."

She hopes you liked this book.

Find her at:
www.leesavino.com

Text copyright © 2018 Lee Savino
All Rights Reserved

No part of this book may be reproduced in any form or by any electronic
or mechanical means including information storage and retrieval systems,
without permission in writing from the author. The only exception is by a
reviewer, who may quote short excerpts in a review.

This book is a work of fiction. Names, characters, places, and incidents
either are products of the author's imagination or are used fictitiously. Any
resemblance to actual persons, living or dead, events, or locales is entirely
coincidental.

www.ingramcontent.com/pod-product-compliance
Lightning Source LLC
Chambersburg PA
CBHW050147110726
47898CB00008B/2703